A Housefly
in
Autumn

Scott Nagele

A Housefly in Autumn

ISBN - 13: 978-1502492951
ISBN - 10: 1502492954

About the Author

Scott Nagele grew up in the Mohawk Valley of New York State. He currently lives in Michigan with his wife and three sons. His other books are; *Temp: Life in the Stagnant Lane* and the story collection, *A Smile Through a Tear*. He also writes a humor blog, "Snoozing on the Sofa" about fatherhood issues.

Scott can be reached at: scott.nagele@yahoo.com

Find out more about Scott Nagele's books at:
www.scottnagele.com

Read Scott Nagele's fatherhood blog at:
www.snoozing**on**the**sofa**.com

ACKNOWLEDGMENTS:

Writing is a solitary sport; publishing is not. Without the help of many generous people, this manuscript would never have been published. I owe a great debt of gratitude to the following people: Janet Harvey-Clark, Linda Oswald, Kathy Prince, Brent Domann, and Jessica O'Brien. Each played a role more important than they probably realize in making this book a reality. I owe special thanks to my always supportive wife, LaRay, and my inspiring sons.

Cover art by
Jessica O'Brien
www.jessieobrienportfolio.blogspot.com
jessieob0908@gmail.com

For my boys, in the hope they will learn to use life's disappointments to grow into good men.

A Housefly
in
Autumn

Anders gasped for breath, but his mouth was below the waterline. He coughed, expelling as much water from his mouth as he could without letting more water in. His lungs burned for a fresh breath of air.

All it would take was a kick of his legs or downward thrust of his arms to raise his head and breathe, but he could no longer feel these limbs, much less move them. Icy water had taken them away. Whether he still had such things as arms and legs was an uncertain point. Only the darkness was certain, and his face was falling down into it.

Something caught him, stopping his descent into darkness. With strained deliberation, it raised him. His nose came out of the water and he breathed. His mouth emerged and he gasped. Air filled his lungs and light shone on his face. With this came a precious streak of hope.

Then the streak of hope began to fade.

He sank again. The unknown force holding him up relented to the power of gravity. Water crept over his mouth. It consumed his nose. The light, with its fleeting hope, was extinguished by the darkness that came wet to his eyes.

His lungs ached for another breath, but there was no way to get it. He stopped sinking, but that which held him did not raise him again. A finger's length below the surface, he was drowning.

It wasn't supposed to turn out this way. Anders wasn't meant to die at 17. There was so much he was supposed to do with his life.

The darkness flooded in, forcing him outside of himself and into a world of limbo as he drifted toward death. This was not the ending intended by his beginning . . .

CHAPTER 1

In the year 1816, on the northern coast of Europe, a man came home from the sea. He'd been away on a fishing ship for many weeks. He would have only a few days to spend at home before he must go back to the sea to earn his living.

The man opened the door of his humble home and quickly passed inside. As he set down his bag, a woman and a little boy ran to him and squeezed him with happy hugs, covering his cheeks with kisses. The woman was his wife and the boy was his son.

When they had hugged themselves out, the woman pressed a coin into the boy's hand and bade him run to the butcher's shop and bring home a fowl so they might have a meal suitable to celebrate the man's homecoming. The boy returned with a plump goose, almost as large as himself, which the woman prepared for their special supper.

After the supper was eaten, and everyone felt satisfied and happy at being reunited, the man lifted the boy onto his knee. "What would you like tonight, my dear little Anders?" the father asked.

Anders made the same reply as always to this question. "Tell me a story, Papa."

The father held the boy at his knee, spinning a fantastic yarn of the sea. The boy sat entranced, his eyes and ears soaking up every word. The story would have made an older boy laugh at its fanciful images and nonsensical plots. At four, Anders was young enough to imagine that everything happened exactly as his father told it.

Anders treasured the tales his father told him. These were the things he missed most when his father went back to the sea, and missing them was what made him feel the most lonely when his father was gone. Then, he would repeat his father's stories to himself in an effort to hold the memory of the man as near to him as he could.

In time, Anders found himself adding details to the stories. This made them more exciting, as if the stories were now great productions he and his father had built together. One day, Anders invented a story all on his own. Now he would have something to tell, next time his father came home.

CHAPTER 2

Anders Christiansen's childhood was similar to that of any other well-mannered boy. He was a happy lad, at ease among other children and mindful of his parents. His boyhood was not lacking in episodes of mischief, but Anders had good reason to avoid misbehavior all he could. While other children might suffer immediate consequences for their misdeeds before their troubles were put behind them, Anders's transgressions were all collected to be re-examined in bulk at his father's next homecoming. Rather than form his own black cloud to hang over the next reunion with his father, Anders kept his clouds to a middling gray by behaving as well as any boy can stand to behave.

The one feature of his childhood that distinguished Anders from the other children was his exceptional talent with words. Anders invented stories that delighted his classmates and teachers alike. He made stories out of everything. If his friend picked up an ordinary stone, Anders concocted an entertaining story about it. He had learned from his father how to paint human personalities onto objects, coaxing his listeners to truly imagine that such listless characters as rocks led interesting lives.

Anders made rocks, spoons, and water buckets speak. It wasn't merely that he said such objects spoke these words or uttered those sounds; he made people believe they heard it for themselves. Anders was imaginative, but so were several of his classmates. The difference was that Anders had a special gift for finding the language to bring his imaginings to life.

At age 14, Anders began to think more of creating stories about people rather than objects or animals. His interest in the lives of real people led Anders to develop a skill for observation. Whenever the opportunity arose, Anders went to the places where people collected. He went to the market and listened to the women bargain for produce. The following day might find him walking the halls of the exchange, watching the businessmen interact. All the while, he kept notes in his head in order to make stories from what he saw and heard.

One evening, after Anders had been out all afternoon observing people in the town square, he came home to find his father sitting at the table. The unexpected visit made Anders's eyes light with joy. "I have a new story for you!" he gushed, even as he hugged his father hello. "It's my best yet. Let me get my papers; I'll read it to you."

Anders rushed off toward the place where he kept his writings, but his father called him back, directing him to sit at the table with his parents. "When I came home today, your mother started to cook some supper, but she was delayed in making a fire in the stove because the wood box was empty."

Anders cast his eyes down. It was his job to fill the wood box.

"She informs me that it is not the first time you have neglected your duties here at home to run off and play in the town."

Anders lifted his head. "But Papa, I don't go to play in town. I go to watch people. All my teachers say I will be a great writer one day. If this is to be so, I must have things to write about. Something adults would write about, I mean. I can't become famous writing children's stories. I must know about real people. That's why I go into town. I want to make something of myself and have you be proud of me."

"I'd rather you be an ordinary man, who remembered his mother and his responsibilities at home, than a famous man who forgot them," his father told him. "If you are meant to be famous, you will be so. You cannot control the future. But you can control who you are. You can let your head be clouded with arrogance and see only glory on the distant horizon, or you can keep it clear to let in the sight of important things that are near to you."

"I'm sorry, Papa. But I only wanted to make you proud." Anders turned to his mother. "And you too, Mama."

Anders's mother spoke. "We are proud of you, because even though you may forget yourself sometimes, above all, you care for your loved ones."

Anders's father tried to keep up his stern face, but this exchange between son and mother made his eyes beam. His wife shook her head. "Look at the two of you," she said, darting her eyes between father and son. "I've never seen a pair of peacocks so proud of each other. Now, go read him your story before he bursts from waiting," she told Anders. "At least you'll both be out of my hair until supper is ready."

CHAPTER 3

When he was 16, Anders finished school. Most of his peers were apprenticed to various craftsmen to learn profitable trades. Anders was chosen to attend the university. A pupil of exceptional talent, he would be trained as a man of letters. His unique skill could not be properly honed among tradesmen. It must be developed through the careful management of scholars.

The university was located in a distant town, making it a tearful goodbye when his parents put Anders aboard the coach, knowing they would seldom see him in the coming years. But it had to be done, for a rare talent of Anders's caliber is not to be wasted. He went to live in that distant town, where it had been arranged that he would pay a modest rent to live in the garret above the home of an old widow.

His arrival at the university advanced Anders's desire to put away his childish stories of talking rocks in favor of tales about the real-life world. Talking rocks were fine for his boyhood mates, but now he was among adults. He could make the most of his talent only by writing stories of real people and their real joys, loves, and sorrows.

This goal he began to pursue immediately, for his head was full of people with just such concerns. He had only been waiting for his chance to let them out. Now, he let them flow onto paper just as they would. When his professors saw the results, they confessed to one another that his gift was of a quality beyond any of their powers to match. It was for them to help him train his gift.

For a year, all went well for Anders. He was a model tenant to old Widow Nielsen, even helping with her household chores in repayment of her kindness to him. His studies progressed beyond the hopes of his professors. He was the ultimate example of an inspired student.

With coaching from his professors, Anders began work on an epic tale that all agreed showed the rough makings of a masterpiece. No one doubted he was, with a few years of practice and polish, on his way toward becoming one of the more famed and respected men of letters in all the continent.

One rainy afternoon, Anders sat in consultation with his mentors when one of the professors broached the subject. "When you become famous, I hope you will not forget about us, we professors who have guided you. We toil in obscurity, wishing only to help gifted men like yourself achieve great things. I hope you will remember us whenever you recount the steps of your pathway to fame."

"I will remember you all, whether or not I achieve great things."

The professor chuckled. "My boy, don't be afraid to show some self-confidence. You have the right to a little vanity."

"With respect, Professor, it seems to me a vain man would never remember you half as well as a modest man would. Believe me, I have been tempted by pride." Anders reflected upon every chore his mother had done for him while he was off studying people. "And every time, pride has tried to make me forget everyone but myself."

"Perhaps vanity is not the right word," the professor agreed. "But you do, deep in your own heart, expect you will be famous one day, don't you?"

Anders gazed out the window into the murky distance. "It is exciting to think of such things as fame and fortune," he said, "but I have learned, through observing people and writing down on paper what I think is the truth of their lives, that it is the difference between what people expect and what really happens to them that makes their stories interesting. If life followed the path we expect, there would be no story in it. It is impossible not to have some expectations for one's own future, but we should never forget that many of our expectations will turn out to have been dreams, only just dreams."

CHAPTER 4

Expectations are only the beginning of any story.

One evening, in his second autumn at the university, Anders was helping Mrs. Nielsen build her cooking fire. A breathless boy came to the door and handed him a letter. The name scribbled on the outside indicated it came from the doctor in the town where Anders grew up. That it came not by the normal post, but by private messenger, hinted its importance.

There were not many words on the paper, yet Anders stared at it for such a long time that the widow grew concerned. "What is it, dear boy? What troubles you?" She took hold of his elbow, and even her light touch would have been enough to knock him off his feet, had she not been quick to guide him into a chair.

Anders still clutched the paper in his hand, but the widow could see it plainly enough. She was not a practiced reader, but the letter was short and it needed only two sentences to tell her everything: *Your father is lost at sea and your mother is gravely ill with grief. It is of vital importance that you return home immediately.*

The next morning Anders boarded the coach for home. He took all of his belongings, as he did not know when, or if, he could return to the university. His mother was without any means of support. He might need to take a job working long hours to provide for her.

As the coach travelled toward home, Anders stared at the passing countryside. It was a beautiful autumn day, yet he saw none of the golden scenes passing before him. His eyes were too clouded with memories. He saw old scenes of himself at his father's knee, listening as fantastic worlds were built up around him. In these worlds dwelt wonderment and adventure, even danger, but he knew he was always protected. He was safe at his father's knee. He had wanted to believe, even after he grew up, that this safe place would always be there for him.

He recalled all the times he had looked up into the eyes of the

9

man he had wanted to become. For a moment he saw those strong, gentle eyes so clearly. Then the vision faded, replaced by the gold and red trees in the distance. The eyes were gone. His father was gone. He was alone on the coach. The only man he could use to mold himself was the very one developing inside of him.

Anders was full of sorrow when he reached home. Yet there were more woes awaiting him. He could not have guessed the severity of his mother's illness. She was confined to her bed, unable to recognize him. Her doctor recounted to Anders how she came to this condition.

"Your father sailed aboard the Sea Star," the doctor explained. "When word first arrived that this ship had gone down in a storm, your mother discounted it as a false rumor. In her determination to prove the news untrue, she went to the docks to make inquiries.

"None at the pier could give her reliable information. Therefore, though the storm still blew, she set out walking to the lifeboat station down the coast. This being a difficult journey for a traveler on foot, she turned up at the station hours later, dripping wet and shivering with cold.

"The men at the lifeboat station had no news of any shipwrecks. The stationmaster begged her to stay until the storm blew out, but she insisted upon returning to the pier to see if any news had come there during her absence. After only a moment in the shelter of the station, she turned back in the direction she'd come.

"In the morning, some dock workmen found her lying near the wharf. She was soaked through and burning up with fever. 'Has the Sea Star come in?' she whispered, though she was half senseless.

"A ship had come in, but it was not the Sea Star. It brought with it three of the Sea Star's crew, rescued from the stormy sea. I'm sorry to say, your father was not among them.

"One of the workmen knew her, so they brought her home and came around to fetch me. I attended her with all my skill, but she has been in the same condition ever since."

Anders found his mother in a miserable state. For two months, he stayed by her bedside, always on watch for some small sign that her health had turned for the better and begging the doctor to leave no remedy untried. Mostly, she was unconscious, but every now and then she would open her eyes and try to speak. He longed to hear her say his name, but all she ever said was, "Has the Sea Star come in?"

On Christmas Eve night, she lay unconscious in her bed. Anders had decorated a fir tree in the corner of her sick room in the hope she might awaken to see it there and be cheered by the spirit of the season. He sat beside her bed, holding her hand and speaking hopeful words to her. There was little chance she heard, but this did not discourage him from trying to convince her to be well again.

He went to the tree and took down an object he had hung as an ornament, bringing it back to the bedside. It was a seashell, painted in many beautiful hues. He held it before his mother's closed eyes. "This is your favorite," he said. "You always smile when you see it, and you tell how Papa made it for you as a memorial of your first Christmas together."

Anders let his chin fall to his chest for a moment. When he raised his eyes back to his mother, he whispered. "Oh, how I wish you would open your eyes and see it now. It would show you how his love for you lives on in this world. Then you could find the strength to stay here with me a while longer." But his mother's eyes did not open.

At length, Anders grew very tired. He set down the ornament on the table beside the bed and was soon asleep in his chair. The noise of some gentle movement from his mother's bed awakened him. At once he was overcome with grief. His first glance told him that his mother had succumbed, and Death, who knows no holiday, had taken her into that unknown land.

After the first wave of grief, Anders noticed something else. The seashell ornament was no longer on the table. It was clutched in his mother's hands, pressed against her heart.

11

CHAPTER 5

In a matter of a few months, Anders had lost both of his beloved parents. It would have been easy for such a young man to give himself over to despair after the double blow he had suffered. He might easily have cast all his hopes and dreams to the winds and buried his talents in their own deep grave.

But this was not the man Anders's parents had raised him to be. For the memory of them, if not for himself, he would be strong. He must honor his parents by doing his best to fulfill their hopes for him.

In a short time, Anders settled his parents' affairs. He sold their humble home, but there was little profit for him in that, having spared no expense in his attempts to make his mother well again. The many debts consumed Anders's entire inheritance. He would need to find some means to support himself.

Anders was determined to try his luck at securing an apprentice position among the local craftsmen when a letter came to him from the university. The message told him that his place at the university was secure. His professors, loathe to lose such a promising student, had taken up a subscription to provide him money for room and board. This being the case, it was an easy decision to return to the university, where he would be welcomed and cared for—where he could, in time, make a way for himself.

Mrs. Nielsen had rented out her garret to a new border. She had no other choice. She badly needed the rent money to live, and she did not know how long Anders would be gone. Even he had no idea if he would ever return to the university when he left for home. It gave Mrs. Nielsen sorrow to know that, on top of all his other troubles, Anders now had to search for a new place to live. Being a tender-hearted soul, she gave Anders warm blankets and the length of floor in front of her hearth until he found suitable quarters for himself.

It was deep winter as Anders started out to find a new place to live. This was an unfortunate time to make such a search. Just as the cold made it uncomfortable, the date on the calendar made it difficult, for all of the livable rooms had been let to students already. All that remained were fearful places in drafty hay lofts and cellars. It was a daunting quest, and he had not many days before the new term began. Anders set out every morning to search, and every evening he returned to the widow's house, cold and still with no room of his own.

After a week, a mid-winter thaw set in. It would not make finding a place to live any easier, but it would make the walking about more pleasant, and that was something. It was impossible not to be cheered by the sunny sky and the warm breeze.

On the second day of the thaw, Anders found a large rock by the lake at the edge of town. The rock had been liberated of snow by the warm sunshine. He sat on the rock, pulled a small bundle from his pocket, and eagerly unwrapped his midday meal. It was not an elegant feast—just some bread and cheese old Widow Nielson had packed for him—but he was hungry and it was a beautiful day to enjoy a picnic.

As Anders took a bite of cheese, he was startled to discover he was not alone. Out of the corner of his eye he spied a large, white dog sitting a few paces away, staring intently at the hunk of cheese in his hand. The dog seemed quite young, yet she was full-grown, or nearly so. Her features were fully formed and she demonstrated none of the awkward movements of a puppy.

Anders did not know what breed she was, but he guessed she was neither all of one kind nor another. Her face combined the intelligence of a shepherd with the melancholy of a hound. Her single outstanding characteristic was that she was completely white.

As he studied his companion, Anders realized the animal showed no signs of aggression. Rather, she hoped to be invited to join his picnic. Anders felt compelled to coax her to the meal, so pitifully did her eyes follow the cheese.

She wanted to move toward him, but her shyness forbade her. She paced, waiting for him to toss some food in her direction. "No," he said softly. "If you want some delicious cheese, you must come here and make friends." His gentle voice seemed to soothe her and she came a few steps closer. He lowered his hand with the cheese down near the ground. "Come on, come get your dinner."

The temptation was irresistible. The wary dog crept in to sniff the cheese in his hand. She gulped it down with eagerness. When she had swallowed the hunk, he slid his hand under her chin and scratched. She liked that. Soon he was petting her head and rubbing her ears. It was the beginning of a long friendship.

For the next five days Anders continued his fruitless search for habitation. Each day he came to sit on the rock by the lake to take his midday meal. The hungry young dog found him there, and the two shared a luncheon of bread and cheese. Every day the dog grew less timid of Anders.

By the fifth day there was no longer any hesitation in her manner toward him. She approached him easily and lingered long after the food was eaten to have her ears scratched and her belly rubbed. At these times Anders could escape the heavy burden of his troubles and ignore the failure of his search. At only this hour every day, Anders knew the comfort of a smile.

CHAPTER 6

On the fifth day Anders gave his friend a goodbye pat on the head and rose to resume his quest. His path took him near the shore, where he could see out over the expanse of ice-covered lake. At this time of year, the lake should be alive with noontime skaters, the people of this region being quite fond of the sport. But after the long thaw, no one dared venture out on the untrustworthy ice. The lake was quiet.

To his dismay, Anders discovered that it wasn't completely silent. Faraway laughter attracted his attention to two small figures on the ice. In spite of the danger, a couple of careless schoolgirls were skating over the weakened sheet. Anders rushed to the water's edge, hoping to warn the girls of their foolishness.

It was too late for warnings. As he approached, the ice gave way and one of the girls disappeared into the lake. The other child let forth a terrible shriek as she raced for the shore.

Anders ran over the ice toward the fresh hole in its midst. As he neared its edge the ice broke beneath his feet, pitching him headlong into the freezing water.

Through the shock of the icy water, he felt his hand brush against something that was neither water nor ice. It was the girl. He drew her into his arms and brought her to the surface. The cold had subdued her senses so she did not panic and struggle against him.

Anders summoned all his strength to push her body up onto the ice surface. The cold water had made him lethargic. He questioned his ability to lift even this small girl. In spite of his doubts, he rolled her onto the ice, pushing her as far back from the water as he could reach.

With the girl out of danger, it remained to save himself. Afraid of imperiling the ice around where the girl lay, he swam to the other side of the opening. This required great labor, as he had very little energy left.

Reaching the far side of the hole, he took a moment to catch his breath; even breathing seemed to require concentration now. Yet he

15

must not wait too long. He could not be sure if he still controlled his legs. With all the strength he could muster, he made the effort to raise himself from the water. Palms flat upon the edge of the ice, he thrust himself upward. He was so heavy. His arms strained.

If he could lock his elbows, he would be able to pitch himself forward, and live. But he was so weak, cold, and heavy. He felt himself sliding backward. For his arms to fail now meant death. Life was a simple matter of raising himself high enough to straighten his arms.

With an effort born of self-preservation he raged against gravity and managed by the slimmest hair to lock his elbows. He need only take a deep breath and pitch himself forward onto the ice. It was in the middle of the deep breath that the ice crumbled under his palms.

Down he plunged, deep into the freezing water. The cold began to make him lose his senses. He meant to kick his feet, but he could no longer feel them. He still held power over his arms though. With them he propelled himself upward. But instead of breaking the surface of the water, his head bumped against a hard place.

Could he have gotten turned around in the mind-numbing cold? Had he hit his head against the floor of the lake? If so it would be the end of him, for he had not enough breath to return to the surface. He felt the hard surface with his hand. It was ice. He had come back up under unbroken ice. With frantic urgency, he searched it with his hands. He had not missed the hole by much, and soon his hands found the jagged edge of the ice. He pulled himself along to the opening and thrust his head out of the water.

For the moment, his burning lungs were rewarded with a sweet draught of fresh air. Yet his trials were far from over. No longer did he possess the strength to drag himself from the water. All he could hope to do was throw his arms onto the ice and hold his head up out of the lake.

His fingers were stiff with cold, and the ice was smooth, so that even the most nimble hands would find no hold. His wet body seemed

16

so heavy. It pulled him down. His hands slid off the ice into the water. He did not sink far this time, as his downward movement was gradual. Even at that shallow depth, it took his last stores of energy to regain the surface.

Now his situation grew worse. When he resurfaced, his back was against the edge of the ice, and he could not turn himself around. Nor did he have the power to keep his head above the water. It swallowed up his mouth and nose for what must be the last time.

All at once, something that seemed no less than the very hand of God caught him. Something, he could not tell what, held him from behind. It did not raise him out of the hole, yet it prevented him from being swallowed by it. By now he did not even possess the composure to guess what it might be that kept him from the depths, for he had passed into a different kind of consciousness.

He perceived neither lake nor ice. All he knew was darkness and light. He was held a hair's-breadth above the darkness, so close that his face fell into it, and he sensed he was suffocating. Then, at last, he was lifted the slightest bit up into the light so that life could be drawn back into him. In the next instant, he was pulled back down into the darkness. Only these vague sensations were his whole world.

Anders had fallen into a world of dreams. Finding his way in that world would be the challenge of his life.

CHAPTER 7

The whole town was abuzz with news of the fantastic story. It was the topic at every supper table. It was told and retold, with varying degrees of color, by the women trading in the marketplace. For a time, it even displaced political debate in the fashionable salons where the town's most important men of business took their daily lunches. It was a heroic tale, which are always fun to repeat, and it was all the more engaging because it seemed to have a happy ending.

"It seems," one corpulent, cigar-smoking businessman began the story, "a young university student—finest specimen of manhood, by all accounts—was passing by the lake when he was shocked to see a poor, helpless child fall through the ice."

"Daughter of the Minister of the Exchequer, that's who she was," put in a skinny, punch-sipping man who was third assistant to the vice mayor.

"True enough, true enough," agreed the fat man. "And a beautiful young flower at that. I have had the great honor of bowing to her on the several occasions when I was in attendance at the Minister's local estate." He added this matter-of-factly, as if it were not at all a gross embellishment of his familiarity with the esteemed family in question.

"A lovely little girl to be sure. I don't suppose she could be more than ten years old," added a young, apprentice commodities trader who had never set eyes on the girl but hoped to imply that he too had seen the Minister's estate up close. "What a horror it would have been to lose her."

"Not to worry." The smoker took a satisfied puff. "Our fearless young hero soon had her lifted up onto the ice where she was safe and sound. But only at his own peril, I must say. Why, the poor lad could not even lift his own bones out of the water."

"Just imagine!" sighed the vice mayor's assistant with a shudder. "Imagine being thrown into such a deadly struggle with the cruel elements."

"Oh I have, I have," responded the rotund man. "Ever since I first heard of it, I have been constantly putting myself, mentally of course, into that dark hole, wondering how I would cope if it were me."

It's well that it weren't, thought the other two simultaneously.

"At any rate," continued the primary storyteller, "now comes the most amazing turn of events. Indeed, it's scarcely creditable. You see, apparently there were two girls skating at the time of the accident, and the unfortunate girl's friend escaped from the ice in time to fetch some men back to the lake for a rescue crew. And when these men got to the lake, do you know what they found?"

"It was the dog," answered the apprentice.

"Yes, quite so. The young lady was lying, cold and terrified, but with no permanent hurt, on the ice where the young fellow had lifted her. Yet the same fellow—and this stretches the limits of belief—was still in the water, quite unconscious. I have that on good authority. And yet he was not lost, for on the edge of the ice lay his dog, teeth firmly clenched 'round the collar of the young fellow's tunic—holding the lad up, you see." He grabbed his own collar as illustration.

"Extraordinary!" gasped the apprentice, as if he were hearing the story for the first time.

"Of course, the rescue party had to quite literally pound the life back into the lad, once they pulled him to the shore. And it is all too likely they would have given him up for dead had not his faithful dog carried on so when they meant to abandon their efforts at resuscitation for lack of any response."

"Yes, that's exactly the same as I heard," interrupted the punch sipper. "The poor rescuers felt menaced by the animal should they attempt to move away from the lad without producing any signs of life. But finally, they did just that, and they were most pleased that the dog had driven them to it. Do you suppose the young fellow shall recover fully?"

"He will. To be sure, he will," replied the large man, taking a confident puff at his cigar. "No doubt the brave, young student will be back at his books before the current term is out. It was a near thing for some little time, but the worst is past. Even now, he is being attended at the Minister's own estate, where, you may be sure, his recovery will be at the hands of only the finest medical doctors in the land."

"They say he has no family or rightful home," added the trader's apprentice. "I was told by a good source that the old widow, on whose floor he had been sleeping, reported his absence to the constable after dark on the day of the accident. That's the only reason his identity was discovered."

"Well, if that is so, he will never be homeless again," concluded the vice mayor's assistant. "You all know how the Minister dotes on that little girl of his. He would do anything for her, and I daresay, he would do much for the one who saved her life. That young man can look forward to a shower of gratitude. And what a man to have in your debt! One can only imagine the Minister's resources."

"Hmm. Yes. Yes." That was all the corpulent man had to say, for a large plate of sausages had just been placed in front of him. He had discovered better employment for his mouth, and one can only guess as to whether he was agreeing to the previous statement or with the arrival of the sausages.

CHAPTER 8

The story of the tragic accident and heroic rescue made its way across town and back again. The men in the salon told the story with surprising accuracy. The Minster's daughter needed only to be dried before a warm fire, fed hot tea, hugged and kissed repeatedly by her parents, and put to bed for a long nap. In a different room, Anders, who needed far more than tea and kisses, lay in bed, attended at every minute by the best medicine of the age, and one large, white dog.

The dog represented the only part of the story told inaccurately in the salon. The storytellers didn't realize the dog had not belonged to the young man. Likewise, the young man didn't yet realize it, but from now on, she did belong to him, and he to her.

It is true that the Minister's daughter, named Suzette, recovered quickly. Within two days of the accident she was her normal, happy self again, though she no longer ran off to skate at every opportunity.

Suzette knew that the man who had saved her was recovering in a bedroom of her house. She very much wished to see him. Everyone was talking about him. He was so brave and strong! She simply must look upon her mighty savior. She begged and begged, but was told she must wait. He must be given time to get well, they told her.

It was not only she who was kept away. Many well-wishers came to congratulate Anders. Each one was turned away by the doctors. The house filled up with gifts and heartfelt notes, but these could not speed the recovery of the young man who had so narrowly escaped death.

Anders was in a poor state to entertain visitors. He slept mostly. When he was awake, he could not set his mind firmly on anything. He knew neither where he was nor how he had gotten there. As hard as he tried, he could not remember anything beyond seeing the two girls skating.

A nurse was stationed outside Anders's room to answer any need he might have. She looked in on him regularly to make certain he did not lack anything helpful to regaining his health. The nurse was a kind

21

woman and she was under strict orders to do everything possible for Anders's comfort.

Whenever Anders felt up to it, he talked to the nurse, who was his only companion. The doctors were too concerned with their work to be good company. The nurse was very patient in answering Anders's questions, which was a great comfort to him, as he could not seem to keep much straight in his mind.

One day, when the nurse brought Anders his broth, he asked her, "Whose house is this?" He had asked her this question more than once before, but he could not remember the answer.

"This is the home of the Minister of the Exchequer," she replied kindly, as if it were the first time she'd told him.

Anders squinted at the far corner of the room and repeated the words softly to himself. "Minister of the Exchequer." He squinted harder. "Do I know him? I feel like I do, but then, I feel like I don't."

The nurse smiled. She had said these same things to Anders two days ago, but she did not mind repeating them. "Of course you know *of* the Minister of the Exchequer. He is a famous man in the national government. But whether you've met him before, I can't say. Perhaps not."

"I don't think I have met him," Anders said. "I can't think of his face."

"I daresay most people haven't actually met him. They only know him from his fame."

"If I don't know him," Anders gazed around the room, "why am I in his house?"

The nurse chuckled. "Because, dear fellow, you are a guest of the Minister. I would even venture to say you are his most valued guest."

"Me? A guest in such a house? How can that be? Why, I'm . . ." Anders shook his head. "I'm just . . ." He squeezed his eyes shut tight, straining to think.

"A university student," the nurse put in.

"Yes," Anders said in a tone between a statement and a question.

The nurse looked away for an instant and cleared something from her throat.

Composed, she turned back to Anders. "Yes, you are a university student, and a rather heroic one at that. And that is why you are the guest of the Minister of the Exchequer. That is why you are the talk of the town, and that is why the next room is full of gifts and greetings for you from all over the country."

Anders stared at her. "I don't understand. All what you just said. I don't understand it."

The nurse patted his shoulder. "I know you don't remember it, but you saved the life of the Minister's daughter. She was skating on the bad ice when she fell through. You went into the water after her and lifted her out. She would have drowned if not for you. And you, yourself, very nearly did drown."

"I don't remember." He looked at his reflection in the bowl of broth on his lap. Who was that man staring back at him? "There's so much, so much I don't remember."

"Patience," the nurse advised him. "You've been through a great trial. Your mind needs some time to catch up. That's all. In time you will be your old self again."

"Yes," he replied. "That's right. That must be right." He looked into her gentle eyes. "How long?"

The nurse cleared her throat once more. She opened her mouth to speak, but whatever words were inside of her were not quite ready to come out.

"How long will I stay in this man's—I can't remember his name—house?" Anders asked.

The nurse let out her breath. "I presume you'll stay here until you are fully recovered. Maybe longer. I expect the Minister will make you his guest for as long as you wish."

"The Minister. The Minister," Anders repeated softly to himself. "The Minister."

CHAPTER 9

As winter was chased away by spring, Anders was deemed well enough to receive one small visitor. The first thing Suzette saw as she entered the east bedroom was the white dog lying on a soft mat on the floor below the bed. The dog watched Suzette walk to the side of the bed, but she did not stir.

The young man in the bed seemed only to notice Suzette at the last moment of her approach. "Good afternoon," she said softly and shyly.

"Good afternoon," he replied, almost as if it were a question.

"I'm Suzette. You saved me from drowning."

"I did? Oh yes, I think I did. The nurse told me about it. I'm sorry, I don't remember it."

"That's all right, I don't remember it so well myself. Mostly I just remember seeing your dog holding you up by your collar."

"My dog? I don't have . . ." His eyes searched the distance as if he were concentrating on making sure his facts were correct. "I don't think I have a dog."

"Of course you do. She's resting down below the bed at this very moment."

His eyes darted around the room, chasing memories that weren't there. "Can you fetch her here?" He need not have asked. The dog, through some canine intuition, sensed that they were speaking of her. She came around to the side of the bed. Anders's eyes widened with recognition as she came into view. "I know you!" he exclaimed. "We ate lunch together." At this sign of recognition the dog threw her front paws on the bed. Anders petted her head.

"Your dog is very pretty," complimented the girl, who was now also stroking the dog's soft fur.

"But she's not my dog." He paused to collect his next sentence. "She's only a stray."

"Well, she thinks she's your dog. They say she guards your bed

24

day and night."

Anders knit his brow. "She's been here? With me? Always?"

Suzette nodded. "She came with you. The doctor wanted to send her away, but Papa said she was your guardian angel. Besides, she's really no trouble. The gardener takes her to feed and walk thrice daily. Otherwise, she lies at the foot of your bed, waiting for you to be well again. She is quite as tame as an angel."

"I didn't know she was there," Anders mused.

"She probably kept quiet because she didn't want to excite you. The doctor said you need your rest."

"But she's just a dog," Anders protested. "How could she know that?"

"Papa says dogs have a special sense for people. They know all about their masters."

"But I'm not her master."

Even as Anders spoke these words the dog rested her chin across his arm.

"She says differently," Suzette corrected him. "And dogs know such things."

Anders made no further protest. He gazed into the dog's warm, brown eyes and thought it might be good, after all, to allow the bond with this dog. She was the only link he had to himself before waking in this room. She was something from before the accident, so terrible that he could not even remember it. This dog was his only friend from a faraway land, the one connection to comfort homesickness for that distant place from which he had come.

Having established this link to his former self, Anders's mind was flooded with memories. "Widow Nielsen!" he exclaimed. "She'll be worried sick! And what of my studies?" His eyes grew wide before his tongue caught up to them. "They must think . . ." In his excitement he struggled to find the right words. "They must think I have quit them all!"

"Don't worry, Anders." The child gave him a reassuring pat on the arm. "The widow and all your teachers know you are here. They have been waiting to visit you. Some of them come by every day. But the doctors have not yet given them permission."

As if he could not hold his worries in his head for more than a moment, Anders moved on to a new question. "How do you know my name?"

She gave a little giggle, seeming to imply the question was a silly one. "Everyone knows your name. You are more famous than the mayor, except none of the grown-ups grumble about you under their breath."

Anders frowned. "Me? How can I be famous?"

"Because you are a great hero. Everyone says so. And I say so the most, because I am the one you saved." Just then, the clock struck the hour. "Oh my, the nurse will give me a good scolding if I stay any longer. It's not your regular nurse today. It's the Sunday nurse."

"The Sunday nurse? I don't remember her."

"Well, that's one good thing for you. She wears the most frightful scowl and her lips are always puckered as if she is just about to kiss some disgusting creature."

Anders made a face. "How unpleasant."

Suzette leaned in toward him and whispered. "Just between me and you, I have an idea about her. I believe she has kissed every frog in the district and is quite put out that none of them had the decency to turn into a prince."

As they laughed about Suzette's theory, they heard approaching footsteps. "That's likely Nurse Kiss-a-Frog now," said Suzette. "I'd better get out of here."

"Thank you for coming, Suzette."

"Thank you for saving me."

All he could think to reply was, "You're welcome."

Suzette exited under the silent scowl of the nurse. When Anders saw the nurse's puffed out lips, he grew profoundly grateful that he was not a frog.

Suzette went to the garden to sit on her bench among the reviving rose bushes. This was her special place, where she went when she had something on her mind that wanted a bit of thought. Today, she thought about the great hero she'd just left. She liked him very much. He was a pleasant person to visit. There was no doubt of that.

Yet he was not at all what Suzette imagined during the time she waited to meet him. She thought he would be more sure of himself, like all the heroes in storybooks. But he was not that way at all. He was shy and uncertain. It was perplexing to have been rescued by such a hero.

In the storybooks, the young damsel seemed always to have her heart swept away by the hero who rescued her. In fact, Suzette had a secret, girlish desire to be smitten with her own hero. Although her hero turned out to be a very nice man, he lacked one important trait. Suzette's hero lacked a heroic demeanor. It might take some deep consideration to figure out how to let one's heart fly to such a hero.

There was yet another thing giving Suzette pause. It was true that everyone knew Anders's name. Everything that could be learned about him had been a topic of discussion. Suzette had overheard things the adults said about him. Consequently, she knew he was a student, and a particularly promising one. That was what confused her.

In the midst of her confusion, Suzette's father came to her. He knew his daughter well enough to understand her reasons for coming to this special place. "Thinking weighty thoughts today?" he asked.

"Not too weighty, Papa," she replied.

"Good. Never burden yourself with heavy thoughts on Sunday. It is a day of rest, after all."

"Yes, Papa," she said, but he could tell she was distracted by a problem on her mind.

Her father sat down beside her. "What are these not-too-weighty thoughts that are sitting on top of your Sunday?"

"I just had my first visit with Anders."

"Oh." He nodded. "He seems like quite a good fellow, doesn't

27

he?"

"Yes Papa. He's ever so nice, but . . ." She looked to the rose bushes for help with her words. "But all the time I was with him, I couldn't help feeling that he wasn't all there. It seemed like a part of him was somewhere else, like it had gone missing or something."

"You must understand, my dear, that he has been very ill. It's to be expected that he is not quite himself yet. We all want to make a great hero of him, but at present, he is only a lad who needs time to recover. There will be plenty of time for the world to fete his heroism once he is fully well again. Let us give him the time he needs before we rush him into living up to our expectations."

"Yes, Papa," she replied, but her eyes said she was not convinced.

"There now, do you feel better about it?"

"I think so." She managed to smile at him. He was at the point of getting up, when she spoke again. "Papa, I have one other question. Everyone in the whole town knows Anders's name, and they are always talking about him. They say he is a university student, and just about the smartest one there is. If all that is true, then why does he speak so slowly and have a more difficult time finding words than the children at school?"

CHAPTER 10

While Suzette was sitting in the garden, arranging her thoughts, Anders was back in his room, trying hard to arrange his own thoughts. For a little while, he was distracted by the presence of the frog-kisser and her bloated lips. By and by, she left, giving Anders a moment of mirth as he imagined her heading straight to the nearest pond.

Then, he was left alone with his memory. The recollections of the widow Nielsen and his studies were only the tip of the iceberg. Now, other memories flooded his mind. Memories, bitter and sweet, made him gasp for breath as they descended upon him one after another.

He remembered his childhood, and the many happy times he had enjoyed as a boy. These were tightly intertwined with memories of his parents. Though the recollection of his parents was associated with many years of happiness, the thread of recall could only end at the tragic loss of both of them.

The loss of his parents hit Anders anew, as if it were fresh news. He wept for them, all the same bitter tears he'd wept when the loss first turned his world upside down. He wept as though the time since then had all been swept away, and he had fallen back to that mournful Christmas Eve.

But the months had not been swept away. As his grief ebbed, they began to fill his mind. He had returned to the university. He'd slept on the widow's floor. He'd been searching for a room to house himself. He had already remembered the dog.

The memory of the lake hit with enough force to push him back into his pillow. The girls were skating. All at once there was a dark gulf in the ice. He ran. He was crossing the ice. It was insanity to stand on this ice, but the girl was drowning. No time to crawl, he must reach her quickly. Just a few more steps and then, and then cold darkness.

Anders recalled how he had to think through every simple action. The cold confused every motion that should have been natural. He'd needed to consider carefully every step in the process of lifting the girl onto the ice. It took such focus of thought to even lift his face out of the water and remind himself to breathe. There is a frightfulness that takes root when natural movements do not come naturally. The horror in that moment made Anders shudder.

Anders shook his head, trying to loosen the memory's hold. The recollections seemed so real and terrifying, yet there was something foreign about them, as if someone else's vivid memories had found their way into his head. They were in his head, so they must be his own memories, but they felt as if they belonged to a different person.

He worked his recollections backward, up out of the ice and back to the university, back to his parents, back to his boyhood. The images were all still there, but they felt strangely borrowed. The core of his memory was himself in some ways, but in other ways it seemed like somebody else. Surely, his own memories belonged to him. That had to be true. Yet, he could not shake the idea that they also belonged to someone who was no longer present.

In spite of how odd Anders's memories felt to him, their return was a step forward. When the doctors discovered this progress, they all agreed it was a promising sign. Anders was permitted to leave his room for short walks in the garden. Suzette joined him whenever possible. The white dog was at his side every time he left the room.

Anders, Suzette, and the white dog grew their friendship as they strolled the garden together. Suzette was pleased to note the progress of Anders's recovery. He could remember the events of his own past almost as well as anyone. This made Suzette happy and lessened the guilt she felt for Anders's suffering as a result of her foolish decision to skate on bad ice.

But Suzette's happiness was not complete. Though Anders could remember old things quite easily now, he still had difficulty arranging his thoughts. He spoke slowly and had trouble finding the right words to use. Even small words sometimes eluded him. At certain times, he could not hold an idea in his head long enough to locate the words to express it.

30

At these times, his vision turned inward, as if he were searching inside himself to find the thoughts that had slipped from his grasp and lay hidden in the tall grass taking root in the back of his mind. When she saw this look come into Anders's eyes, Suzette stifled a shudder of guilt.

The white dog took no notice of Anders's struggles. She was ever at his side and always content to be there. Anders had been kind and gentle to her from the first moment of their meeting, and he was the same now. She cared not whether his mind were brilliant, average, or a bit slow in its evolutions. She cared only that his heart was good, his touch soft, and his voice gentle. She was devoted to him, no matter the results of his recovery.

One day Suzette came to Anders breathless with anticipation. "Hurry. Put on your shoes," she commanded. "I have a surprise for you."

"Oh? What is it?" Anders asked.

"Don't waste time with questions when you could be putting on your shoes." The impatient girl brought his shoes to him. "I'll show you."

When Anders was ready, Suzette led him through the garden to a charming little cottage on the other side of the estate. The girl hurried him to the door and threw it wide open. Inside was the most beautiful little house Anders had ever seen. It was small by comparison to every other building on the Minister's estate, yet it was larger than the house in which Anders had grown up.

The rooms of the cottage were outfitted with everything necessary for the inhabitant to live a comfortable life. There were cozy chairs, lush rugs, and an ample hearth for keeping away the chill of winter nights. Large windows let in bright, cheerful sunshine. In the bedroom stood a bed fit for a king—long and wide, with fluffy, eiderdown pillows.

Another room housed an immense desk, well-stocked with bottles of ink and pens. Empty shelves waited to be filled with books. Ornate lamps would light the room when darkness fell.

"Well, what do you think of it?" Suzette asked at the end of the tour.

"It's beautiful," Anders replied with a sincerity born of awe.

Suzette looked crestfallen. "Is that all?"

"It's *very* beautiful." Anders struggled to find sufficient words to satisfy his friend. "It's the most beautiful house I've ever seen."

"That's more like it." Suzette's form straightened with renewed pride.

"Who lives here?" Anders asked.

Suzette became coy. "You don't know?"

Anders searched his memory. Should he know? Had he been here before? Of course not. He'd had no occasion to visit such a splendid home before. "Truly, I don't," he said at last, a little afraid he would disappoint her again.

Suzette was not disappointed. Her childish excitement burst out. "Why, you live here, silly!"

Anders gave a start. Was this true? What did it mean? Did he really live here? Was there a whole part of his life that he still did not remember? A wave of panic came over him. "No. No. No," was all he could stammer.

Suzette couldn't sense his panic over her own excitement. "Of course you do," she explained. "This is Papa's guest house, and you are Papa's guest. You are to live here for as long as it pleases you."

Anders caught his breath. "Then, I have not lived here before?" he whispered in his relief.

"What? Oh no, of course not. You've not been here before. How you do confuse me sometimes!"

Anders dropped into one of the comfortable chairs. "But, I am to live here now?"

Suzette beamed at him. "Of course you are. Isn't that what I have just told you?"

"Yes?" Anders pondered. "I think it is."

Suzette leapt over Anders's confusion. "Isn't it wonderful? Papa had the workmen refresh the whole house for you. And because you are a student, he made the back room into a study for you. You'll have a proper place to work on your lessons and plenty of room for all the schoolbooks you could ever need."

Anders began to feel the weight of the Minister's generosity on his humble shoulders. "He did all of this? For me?"

Now Suzette's excitement gave way to a humble sincerity of her own. "He would give you anything you want, to repay you. I would do the same." For an instant her eyes fell and her foot painted awkward circles in the fabric of the rug. "But I know I could never repay you enough."

CHAPTER 11

Though the cottage was as inviting an abode as he could imagine, Anders made excuses to delay moving into it. Meanwhile, he asked for an audience with the Minister of the Exchequer. The Minister was away, tending the finances of the state, and several days passed before Anders was able to speak to him.

Finally, the Minister returned and Anders was brought forthwith to the main house. The Minister received Anders in his office, a huge room, with an enormous desk and walls lined with journals containing important documents of the state. Anders was timid about entering a place of such official importance, but the Minister beckoned him so earnestly that he stepped over his fears and presented himself before the Minister's desk.

The Minister bade Anders to sit and offered some refreshment, but Anders was too nervous to take anything more than a seat. "You look well," the Minister said. "I congratulate you on the progress of your recovery."

"Thank you," Anders replied, perched on the edge of his chair.

A moment of silence followed. Satisfied that Anders had finished making his reply, the Minister began again. "I'm pleased you are well enough for us to finally speak, man to man. Until now, there has been so much concern for your health that I haven't had the opportunity to look you in the eye and express my gratitude for all you have done for me and my family."

Though the Minister paused, Anders knew not what to say, so he said nothing.

"Your humility matches your courage," the Minister continued. "I will try not to embarrass you too much. But the fact remains; you've done a service for my family that cannot ever be repaid. You have my deepest gratitude. I am ever in your debt."

Anders was bewildered by this statement. He had no words ready with which to answer. "Thank you," he whispered.

The Minister chuckled. "Perhaps we will speak of this again, at a time when your humility is off its guard and my gratitude can sneak past it."

Anders was lost. "Yes, sir," he replied.

The Minister smiled, shaking his head the tiniest bit. "But you have come to speak to me. Perhaps there is something you need. Only say the word. What is it?"

Anders leaned forward. "Suzette." He cleared his throat, for he could hardly hear the word himself. "She took me to the cottage."

"Do you find it unsuitable? Is there something lacking? It can be altered to meet your needs."

"I . . . I have not . . . I don't live there."

"You need not delay," the Minister assured him. "The house is ready to be occupied, and the doctors have given their consent."

"But," Anders stammered, "I cannot pay. The professors give me an allowance. It is hardly enough for an attic room. I can't afford such a house."

This time the Minister nodded as he smiled. "Dear, dear, boy. Is this what's troubling you? You're worried about money? If I have my way, you will never have such a worry in your lifetime. There is no rent. The house is yours to live in for as long as you like. It will never cost you anything, should you live to be an old man in it, and it is only the least part of my gratitude to you."

"It's too much," Anders argued. "I need only a roof and a floor to live."

The Minister ceased smiling. "Too much?" His eyes looked far away and it seemed as if a mist had spread over them. "You've no idea what you've done, do you? Suzette is my only child. She is the only child I shall ever have. To her mother and me, she is the entire world. She is the light that shows us the way. Fate was near the point of snuffing out that light, taking the whole of our world away from us. You are what stands between us and a world filled with darkness. You might have ended your own life in doing so, but you gave us our light

35

back. You gave us our very lives. For that, nothing is too much. What you call too much is nothing to me. Everything would be nothing without the light of my life. I beg you, honor your selfless actions by living in the cottage. Tell me all of your needs; they will be met. There is nothing you could ever want that is more valuable than that which you have given me."

The Minister's words came at him in such a flurry that Anders could grab hold of none of them in order to form a response. Yet the spirit of them wrapped itself around him. He wished to say something sympathetic to the Minister's outpouring, but his throat was tightened by the force of the sentiment behind the words. He felt tears forming in his eyes. To hide them, he bowed in acquiescence to the Minister's request.

And so Anders took up his residence in the beautifully kept guest cottage, a short walk from the main house. The white dog moved into the guest cottage with Anders, who had come to embrace the idea of having a dog of his own to care for.

It was fortunate he felt this way, for the dog had already decided that it would be so. She had watched over him like a jealous mother throughout his recovery, and now the price she expected was that she be allowed to shower him with unconditional love for all of her life. Anders counted this a reasonable bargain and accepted her terms.

Thus, they became housemates, and Anders began thinking of a name for her. He thought a long time, and finally began to call her Elsa. It was a pretty name, he thought. It suited her well. Now that she had a name, they could truly be the best of friends.

CHAPTER 12

At last, Anders was ready to return to his studies. The doctor who attended his recovery advised him to forgo the current term and begin fresh in the next. He had not known Anders before the accident, but he'd heard many things about the student's intellectual potential. The man he doctored over the past weeks did not fit the description of the person about whom he'd heard all those things.

In spite of the doctor's pleas to take more time to recover, Anders was insistent; he was tired of being cooped up all day. There was no physical reason why he shouldn't return to the university, so he would not be stopped.

Having settled into his new home, Anders's first act was to call at the widow Nielsen's house to assure her of his well-being. This done, he found himself with no business left that should interfere with the resumption of his studies. The term had several weeks remaining, and he did not relish the prospect of remaining idle for all that time. It would be better to get back to his normal routine as soon as possible.

His professors were delighted to see him. They pumped his hand and congratulated him on his heroism. One was not offered the chance to mentor such a promising student more than once or twice in a lifetime, so it was a great relief to find him back within the halls of higher learning. They all breathed easier and walked with lighter steps when they caught sight of him, for it meant that their careers, as well as his, were rescued from the doldrums.

Yet, after speaking with him, they cast uncomfortable glances at each other. None could put his finger on exactly what was the matter. All feared even to speculate. At length, they convinced themselves it was just an awkward reunion and all would be well once Anders could get back to work. To that purpose, they gave him the finished portion of his manuscript to review so it would be fresh in his mind. Then they could meet and decide in which direction to best proceed. This done, each went his own way, repeating in his mind, "All will be well. All will be well."

Anders was left feeling out of sorts by the reunion as well. Was he truly the person he remembered himself to be, or had he become someone else? Of course, he was the same. Someone else could not remember the events of his life. Only he, the same person he ever was, could recall his own childhood, even if those memories seemed more distant and hazy than they used to be.

"Oh, it's only that my brain has been asleep for so long," he told himself. "When it has had time to exercise, I will feel better." Still, the manuscript he had been given made him uneasy. It was the work of his mind at its best. Despite his reassuring words to himself, he feared the comparison.

By now, Anders had become more familiar with the Minister and his wife. He had already become fast friends with Suzette, and that friendship allowed him to feel more at ease with her parents. Having no more family of his own, the interest this new family took in his well-being was a comfort to him.

Anders had grown quite comfortable enough to begin taking his supper at the family's table with them. After all the unhappy events he had suffered, it was a daily reminder of past happinesses to share this meal with them. Nothing could change the past, but such moments could make the present a little better.

Anders put the manuscript from the professors on his desk and went to take supper in the house with the family. Supper was a good excuse to put off his work for a while. There would be time enough for that later. For now, he needed the comfort of those who loved him.

The Minister and his wife were eager to learn of Anders's return to the university. "How did it go today?" the Minister asked.

"Well," Anders replied. "It went well." But he didn't know if he believed it.

"You must have been so very pleased to reacquaint yourself with your professors," the Minister's wife added.

"Yes, I was," Anders said. "Very."

"And I bet they were so proud of you," she continued.

"They welcomed me very kindly," Anders said.

The Minister smiled and shook his head. "Always so modest. I bet they fell over backward with joy at the sight of you. You are their star pupil. Your work means as much to their careers as it does to your own."

Anders bowed his head down. He felt a twinge of panic crawl up his spine.

The Minister's wife took note of Anders's demeanor. She chided her husband. "Gustav, please. Don't speak of his professors with such disrespect. Can't you see it upsets him?"

"Oh, pshaw! I meant nothing by it. It was merely harmless table talk." He turned his attention toward Anders. "You see that, son, don't you? I meant no harm."

Anders raised his head slightly. "Yes, sir," he said softly.

"You see, my dear, there's nothing to it," the Minister said to his wife. "It's no denigration of his professors to speak of the excellence of the student who shares our table with us."

With every reference to him or his work, Anders felt the fear grow within him. His knees began to shake. His face felt hot. "What are the flowers that border the guest cottage?" he blurted out before anyone could make mention of those fearful topics again.

Everyone took pause at this sudden change of topic. At last, the Minister considered the question. "The flowering shrubs, you mean? I believe they are yellow azaleas. "

The truth was that Anders did not know what he meant. He had hardly noticed the bushes near the cottage. Nevertheless, he nodded. "Yes. That's what I mean. The shrubs."

"Do you like the azaleas?" the Minister asked. "Would you like more of them?"

Anders did not care about azaleas, but talking about flowers was not at all frightening. "Yes, I like them very much," he said.

"Very well. I will send the gardener to consult with you. You may direct him to plant azaleas anywhere you wish."

"Thank you," said Anders. He felt better now.

They did not speak of azaleas for the rest of the meal, but they did not mention Anders's career at the university either, and this was all that mattered to the young man.

After supper, Anders and Suzette distracted themselves with a capital game of hide and seek. Elsa joined in with them, which might have made the game unfair, since Elsa could quite easily find either of them with her nose. Yet Elsa stayed at Anders's heels the entire time, letting him take the lead in everything, and not once giving the least clue as to where Suzette might be hiding.

It began to grow dark and Suzette was called in for the evening. Anders was left to face his manuscript. He went back to his cottage, resolved to begin the work before him, but not the least bit eager.

"Oh well," he thought, "the sooner I begin, the sooner things will get back to normal." He picked up the papers and began to read. The fear at the back of his mind turned to terror almost immediately. In the very first sentence was a word he could not place. He turned it over and over in his mind, trying to bring forth the meaning from it. No matter how he tried, he could not make the word mean something to him.

Surely this was a mistake—the wrong manuscript. He turned back to the cover page. There was his name clearly written, and the title. It was the title he had carefully chosen for his master work. He went back to the word he did not know. He stared at it—the word he had once easily called to mind.

But there was much to read. He must go on. The meaning of the word would come to him in time. It would. It must.

He read on. There were more words he had to pass over. They soon became the smaller of his troubles. He recognized the characters and the line of the plot, but he could not predict the next page. To what end was the plot advancing? He did not know. He could not imagine. Why did the characters say certain things? He did not know.

Why did they do this or that? Again, he knew not.

"I must know the reasons for these things," he chided himself, "I wrote them." Yet he often found himself asking, "What did *he* mean in writing that?" There were three days until his next meeting with his professors. In that time he studied the manuscript with little sleep and little to eat, all to no avail. When the time appointed for the meeting arose, he went to see the professors looking worn and haggard. He could hardly keep himself from shaking.

CHAPTER 13

There were three professors in the room with Anders. Two were well into their middle years. One of the two was becoming bald. The other was even more so. The less bald of the two wore eyeglasses that were too small for his head and seemed to pinch his large nose. The more bald one had perfect eyesight.

The third professor in the room was older than the others. He had a full head of gray hair, reasonably good eyesight, and a white beard. Anders had worked closely with all three for more than a year. He had grown to know them well. But now they seemed like strangers. Today, they were more like the members of a jury, waiting to pass down a terrible judgment upon him.

After they had exchanged greetings, the older professor suggested they take seats around a square table. "I can't tell you how happy we are to have you back with us," he told Anders after they were seated.

"I am happy to be back with you," Anders replied.

"We've been eager to resume advising you on your manuscript," said the more bald one, as the less bald one nodded in agreement.

"I have also been eager." Anders's voice was very soft.

"Good!" exclaimed the less bald. "Then let us waste no time. Tell us your ideas about Hans."

"Hans?" Anders knew Hans was the man he had written about in his manuscript, but he had nothing in mind to say about him.

"Yes, Hans, the main character of the work."

Anders did not reply. There was only one thing he could think of to say, but he knew it was not the answer to the question. They wanted some secret about Hans that only he could know. But Anders knew no secrets about Hans. All Anders knew about Hans were some things he had read in the manuscript they'd given him, and these he could not keep straight in his mind.

Three pairs of eyes prodded him. Still he could think of nothing else, so he said what was in his mind, though there was no hope this would satisfy them. "Hans is a fisherman."

"Of course he's a fisherman." The less bald professor made no effort to conceal his impatience. "He has been a fisherman since page one. What we wish to know is how you plan to further develop his character. What enlightening incidents will befall him?"

"There will be some enlightening incidents. Certainly there will be some." Anders only wished to assuage the professor's frustration. He hardly knew what he was saying.

"Come now," insisted the more bald one, "don't hold back on us. You must have some plots in mind."

"I can't say," whispered the student, finding himself caught in the steady gaze of the older professor. This one had not yet asked a single question. He'd only watched the exchange with kind but inescapable eyes. "I can't say just now."

"What? Have you secrets from us, after all this time?" asked the less bald one.

"No, no. It's just that I haven't thought of them, I haven't thought them out."

"Very well, what about Hans's wife then. Thus far you have done a masterful job of showing us his strengths and weaknesses through her eyes. What insight will she give us in the future?"

The old professor's gaze would not let him hide. It followed him as he tried to disappear behind every false answer. Running away was becoming too difficult a game. He could not outrun those eyes. He could only stand and face them. "I don't know," he said.

"What do you mean?" The less bald one pushed his eyeglasses up over the bridge of his nose. "You must have some ideas. We cannot advise you properly if you will not share your ideas. What are they?"

"Whatever you want them to be! I don't know!" Anders cried. The two younger professors, having leaned further over the table with each question, flew backward into their chairs, taken off guard by the extreme loudness of the reply. Perhaps they would have been angered by this show of disrespect had they not noticed the stream of tears flowing down their student's face. Neither knew how to respond. As they began forming the first words for a feeble attempt, the old professor held up his hand to stop them.

Instead, it was he who spoke. "Let us say no more about the manuscript for now. Anders, you have endured much. I fear that we, in our own eagerness, have rushed you into resuming your labors. You need time to recover yourself. It was our error, not yours. On behalf of us all, I beg your pardon." He bowed slightly to show his earnestness. "Now, go. Breathe some fresh air and think nothing of this meeting. When you wish to meet again, you need only come to me. I will be waiting. I will be waiting patiently. I will listen to whatever you need to say. And if you need to remain silent, I will listen to that as well."

After Anders had left, the bald professor took the manuscript from the table. "Oh my, he left this behind. What shall we do with it?"

"That is a relic now," replied the old professor. "You may lock it in your cupboard and throw away the key."

"But he must have it to review. Else, how will he ever resume it?"

The old one looked out the doorway through which Anders had left. "How will he ever resume his own life? That is what we should wonder."

Chapter 14

The next afternoon, the doctor who had attended Anders through his recovery came to visit him. He found Anders outside, lying on the lawn, watching the clouds. His dog lay beside him, her head resting atop his chest. To all the world, the two of them appeared to represent a picture of happiness. A great artist could not have painted a scene of equal tenderness.

"What luck," exclaimed the doctor as he approached. "I feared you would be at the university today and I would miss you."

"No," replied the young man, still watching the clouds. "I did not go there today."

"In that case, will you oblige me in making a quick examination of you? I promise, it will take but a moment. Then you may return to your thoughts."

"You should not promise what you cannot deliver."

"But I assure you, it will take no time at all."

"No, I don't mean that." Anders had yet to look away from the sky. "Don't promise that I may return to my thoughts." Anders pressed his teeth into his bottom lip for a moment before he said more. "They say you are the best doctor that is to be had, and I believe it." Anders's eyes followed a puffy, white cloud as it meandered toward a distant edge of sky. "I believe you are the best doctor. But even you cannot promise that I may return to my thoughts."

"I'm afraid I do not take your meaning," the doctor said.

Anders turned his head toward the doctor. "Do you know what I have been doing here, all day long?"

The doctor shrugged. "Up until now, I would have guessed you were enjoying a beautiful spring day."

"I have been trying to return to my thoughts." Anders turned his attention back to the cloud he had been following. "Doctor, have you ever been thinking about something—really thinking hard on it—and then been interrupted?" He bit his lip again. "Then, when you try to go

45

back to it, you can't find it again? You might get near it, but you can't ever get back to what it really was—the true thing you were thinking about, I mean."

"Yes, of course, everyone has lost their train of thought at one time or another."

"That thought I can't get back to is *all* my thoughts." Anders caught his breath as though he were winded. "I have lost my train of life."

The doctor was not insensible to the meaning of these words. One does not become the best physician that is to be had without knowing something of the workings of the mind. In fact, he had been the first to notice Anders's sluggish mental recovery and it concerned him. He hoped time would cure it, but even he could not be sure. There was nothing for him to do but try to infuse hope into Anders, for there was no solution in medicine.

"The mind is more complex than the body," the doctor began. "Sometimes it needs more time to heal. You might find improvement at any moment. But let us first be certain the body has healed. Come, let me have a look at you."

Anders felt sincerity in these words and did as he was bade. He slid out from beneath Elsa's sleepy chin and rose so the doctor could give him a good looking over. This was done in silence, except for an occasional instruction from the doctor. At length, Anders asked the question the doctor had been anticipating. "Do you really believe I'll get better in time?"

"You say they told you I was the best doctor to be had. But there is a better doctor. His name is Time. He's the best doctor I know. That much I will tell you. But I cannot speak for him. We can only wait and see what he can do. Have faith in him, and in yourself, and you will put yourself in the best possible position." He patted Anders on the back. "There now, we're done. You are as fit as any man I know."

Anders turned to face the doctor. If there were not a tear running down his cheek, there might as well have been. "Doctor, what's wrong with me?" The words were almost too heavy for his tongue to force out.

The doctor thought for a moment before he answered. "The truth, Anders, is that even with all my training and experience, still, I can only guess what is affecting you. When those men pulled you from the water, every one of them concluded you were drowned. It was only your friend here," he motioned toward Elsa, "who knew better, and that was only by an instinct we will never understand. There was no science in it. What we men of science do know is that the brain needs air to function properly. When a man is so nearly drowned that all about him think him dead, it may be that his brain has suffered from a lack of that precious substance."

"But, will I get better?" the desperate youth demanded.

"The problem lies in the fact that I cannot look into your head to see what damage has been done, or predict if it will heal itself. I know this is not a satisfactory answer, but you must be patient. Only time will answer. In the meanwhile, exercise your mind as you would a recovering limb, for you have more power over what happens now than does any doctor. Arrange your thinking toward the best possible result."

"If I could arrange my thoughts, I wouldn't need any answer," Anders snapped back in anger. "What good is your medicine, if I must wait for time to answer? Time goes on forever. I can't wait forever."

The doctor's posture stiffened in response to Anders's outburst. "Anders, you must listen to me," he said. "Sometimes medicine can do miraculous things for people. Sometimes it can do nothing. In this past week, I have seen a man, who seemed only mildly ill at first, waste away before my eyes. All of my medicine could do nothing to save him. He died. In that same time, I have treated a boy who seemed to be at the threshold of death's door. He is nearly fully recovered now, thanks to medicine. There is a higher power that decides the lives of men. Medicine is only a tool, used to carry out these decisions."

"If medicine can do nothing on its own, why did you bother to come?" Anders hissed through clenched teeth.

Putting a hand on Anders's shoulder, the doctor looked earnestly into the young man's eyes. "Anders, it is nothing short of a miracle that you are alive today. If you had seen as much of death as I have, you would know that. Whatever may come to you, remember, you have your life. Cherish the life that was given back to you. It was given back to you for a reason. We may never know why, but there is a reason. Live your life; don't waste it in self-pity. Fulfill that reason."

The doctor bid farewell to Anders and Elsa. As he walked away he rubbed the corner of his own eye. Even for one who had seen so much of death, his heart was not hardened. Though he had needed to be a bit stern with the lad, Anders's fears touched his very soul, more so because they mirrored his own fears about the young man's future.

CHAPTER 15

That evening, and the next after that, Anders took his supper alone in his cottage. He did not return to the university. In spite of this, he sent word to the main house that he was very busy with his studies and would prefer to have his supper brought to him. He did not like to mislead the family that sheltered him, but he felt completely unable to face them over the supper table. He wanted only to be alone with his troubles, for as long as it took to understand what to make of himself.

Anders spent these days walking with his devoted dog through the expansive gardens or lying on the grass, gazing at the sky. He was, all at once, lost within and without himself. Elsa could do little to help him find his way, but her constant presence told him she would go wherever his path should lead.

On the second evening, Suzette visited him after supper. She found him on the grass, halfheartedly arranging the border of a flower bed. "Why don't you come to the house for supper?" she asked. "We all miss you."

"I don't know. I think I like it here. It's quiet."

"And you need the quiet to study? You've been studying terribly much these last few days. They must give you very difficult lessons to learn at the university."

Anders nodded. "They do." He'd been studying the very difficult lesson they had given him at the university ever since his last visit, but he had yet to make any headway against the problem of what to do with it.

"I don't think I would like the university," she said. "I don't like to study so much. I prefer to be with my friends, like you and Elsa. I suppose you enjoy the studying though."

He made a sound that seemed like a chuckle at first, but he didn't smile like people usually do when they chuckle.

"I wish you would at least come to play hide and seek with me," she told him. "I like playing with you better than the boys at school.

49

Some of them try to kiss me when they find me."

"I don't feel much like playing."

There was silence. Finally, her childish impatience got the better of her. "Why are you so sad?" she asked quietly.

"I don't know." He could hardly have begun to tell her why.

"I know," she said without any childishness in her voice. "You're sad because you talk so slowly now." Her words took the breath out of him, for they hit a complex target very simply. The pain of that simple truth would not allow him to respond.

"I was thinking about you in school today," she continued. "I was thinking about all the things I heard people say about you. How you were the best pupil at the university, and how all your teachers thought you were a genius. I couldn't figure it all out, because nobody ever called Mama or Papa a genius, or any of my classmates, but they all talk without so much effort as you. I couldn't understand it. But then," she paused and swallowed hard, "I remembered seeing you there in the water with Elsa just barely holding you up, and I realized you didn't always speak slowly." It was growing dark, and her back was toward him, yet he could tell by her voice she was crying. "I figured it out. You lost your genius when you saved me." Her sobs would not be stifled. "I'm so sorry. You must hate me."

With those words she shifted the focus of his pity from himself onto her. He went to her and put his arm around her shoulders. "How could I hate such a pretty flower?" he asked.

"I'm not a flower. Flowers don't hurt people. I'm just a silly, selfish girl. Do you know what I thought when I first heard you speak? I thought you were having such a difficult time because you weren't completely thawed out yet. You know, how when it's autumn, and you see the last housefly of the year, and you can easily catch it in your hand because it's too cold for it to move quickly? That's what I thought was wrong with you. I thought you only needed to be warmed up for your words to speed up. But now I can feel your hand on my shoulder. You're just as warm as anybody, but your words are still slow. Can you believe I actually thought your voice was frozen? Have you ever known a pretty flower to hold such silly ideas as that?"

"I know nothing of the ideas of flowers, but I'm glad you told me yours. I don't think it's silly at all. I think it's sweet. You have a good heart."

"But you don't know the worst part." She let her head hang low. "If I truly had a good heart I could wish you had let me drown instead of injuring yourself to save me. But I can't do it. I don't want to be dead. And when I think of how Mama and Papa would cry, I just can't wish you had let me drown. I must be the most selfish person in the world."

He gave her a gentle shake of his head. "Now you *are* being silly. Everybody wants to live. It's not selfish." He smiled at her and she smiled back through her tears. "You cannot change what's already happened, so don't feel bad about it. Besides, if you were drowned, who would I have to play hide and seek with?"

She threw her arms around him to give him a long hug that was nine parts relief. "Will you truly play hide and seek with me again? Even after all the hurt I've caused you?"

"Tomorrow, I will come to the house for supper," he assured her. And then we shall play the finest game of hide and seek that has ever been played."

CHAPTER 16

True to his word, Anders took supper in the main house the next evening. Later, he and Suzette played hide and seek as promised. They played all manner of fun games through the whole summer. Wherever Anders was, Elsa could be found close by.

Playing games with Suzette and Elsa brought the first truly happy times Anders had enjoyed in many months. Ever since the previous autumn, his life had consisted of one strife upon another. But when he chased Suzette and Elsa through the gardens, he lived childhood joys again. In moments of solitude, his difficulties might once more crowd his thoughts, but his friends provided some relief to his troubled mind. His woes could not block out the sun while Suzette and Elsa were at hand.

Likewise, Anders's company made Suzette's days light and happy. In no time at all, he grew to become her best friend. She found it easier to talk and play games with him than with children of her own age. He did not stand off from her like the girls did, because of her cleverness and her family's elevated rank. Nor did he attempt to play pranks like the boys were wont to do.

Anders was just somebody who was fun to talk to and play games with. When she bested him at some game, he did not sulk and pretend to be unlucky. When he led her somewhere by the hand, she could be sure he was not taking her someplace to frighten her with gruesome sights. She always knew she could trust Anders, and that made him a true best friend.

Suzette was still a child, and could lose herself in childish joys during summer, but Anders was not a child. Though not yet 18 years old, he was the master of his own fate. The weight of responsibility for his future forbade him to think of only childish things. Every day, he felt more and more guilty about allowing his new family to believe he was working at his studies when he had not done a single thing to advance them. He was taking advantage of the Minister's kindness, while doing nothing with his own hands to support himself.

The more Anders thought about his situation, the more daunting it seemed. Growing hopelessness sapped him of the ambition needed to take charge of his future. He could often be found lying on the grass near his cottage with Elsa, letting the weight of his troubles root him to the ground.

On one such occasion, a voice startled him from his reverie. "I suppose your professors go easy on you in summertime." Throwing a glance over his shoulder, Anders was embarrassed to find the Minister of the Exchequer approaching.

He hurried to his feet. "Yes, sir," he replied, feeling the necessity to say something. Inwardly, he winced. Out of reflex he had lied to the man who deserved the utmost respect, hence the truth, from him.

"I've come to see how you are settling in," the Minister said as he came up to Anders, "and to see if there is anything else you require for your new home."

"Oh no," Anders assured him. "It's quite more than I need. Won't you come inside?"

Inside the cottage, the two of them sat opposite each other. The Minister looked around him at the visible parts of the house. "I hope you are comfortable here. We can have anything altered to suit you."

"Oh no, Minister. It's quite comfortable as is."

"Please, call me Gustav," the Minister insisted. "You've earned that right."

"It's perfectly comfortable as it is, Gustav," Anders repeated. He swallowed hard at pronouncing the Minister's name; that friendly little kindness made his deception weigh heavier.

"I'm glad to hear it," Gustav said. "I hope Suzette isn't distracting you and taking up all your time with her games."

"No, sir." The word sir seemed like a fair way to avoid having to call him by his given name. "She is nothing but a comfort to me."

"Good. Then I won't worry about your situation. If you have need of anything, you will, of course, merely say the word."

"You are too kind to me," Anders said. It was true. The Minister was too kind to be deceived any longer. Anders let his head fall into his hand and looked down at the floor. "I have lied to you. I have not seen my professors in weeks."

Gustav sat still. "I see," he said in a calm voice.

"I'm not up to the work anymore. I don't know if I ever will be."

In the pause Anders left for the Minister to voice his ire, Gustav said nothing. Anders could not make himself look up at the man, but he imagined there must be a prominent scowl covering his face.

"I have taken advantage of you for too long," Anders said. "I will leave as soon as you wish."

"Nonsense," replied the Minister. "You have taken advantage of no one, and you will stay as long as you want." Anders slowly raised his eyes to find anything but a scowl on Gustav's face. "Besides," the Minister went on, "I have consulted with your professors. I know you haven't been at the university. So, if it comes down to deception, we are even on that score."

"You knew?"

"Yes."

"And yet, you let me stay here?"

"Of course I did. I thought we had settled the matter already. You have earned your place here, regardless of the future. That will never change."

"But I have become useless," Anders moaned. "I can't lean upon your gratitude forever. I have nothing of value to offer."

"You are a great friend to all of us," Gustav volunteered. "Let that be enough."

"Let me labor on your behalf. Let me be your house servant, your errand boy. I may not have much of a mind, but I have hands. Let me earn my keep with them."

The Minister began to reiterate that Anders need do nothing to earn his keep when the depth of the pleading in Anders's eyes stopped him. It was out of the question that this young man should end up as a house servant. Yet, maybe there was someplace where they could find a satisfactory arrangement. "As I recall, you seem to enjoy the flowers and shrubs of the grounds."

"Yes, the gardens are very comforting to me."

"In that case, I propose to employ you as assistant groundskeeper. It is hard work, but I think it is work you can enjoy. Meanwhile, you will be offering something of undisputed value in exchange for your residence. When you decide to return to the university, we will make whatever alterations to the arrangement that are appropriate. Does this suit you?"

Anders exhaled relief. "Yes, sir. It suits me very well."

Finally understanding what it was that Anders most needed from him, the Minister added another layer of it. "I warn you. I am very particular about the appearance of the gardens. I will expect you to be diligent in learning your trade and conscientious in executing it."

Gustav had never seen a relaxed smile like the one he saw spread across Anders's face. "Oh yes, sir. I will."

"I'm glad to hear it." He leaned forward in his chair but did not rise. "Now there is one more thing I want to say. You called yourself useless. Well, I don't believe it. Nevertheless, I am not going to sit here and tell you over and over again that you are not useless. You will not believe me anyway. You will only believe in your own worth when you have proven it to yourself. Maybe working hard in the gardens will prove it to you. Maybe it will have to wait until the day you return to your studies. I don't know. What I do know is that you are a very young man. You have a long time ahead of you, and in that time you will accomplish the things that will make you believe in your own value. The sooner you believe, the better off you will be. I advise you to stop dwelling on your perceived uselessness and start looking for the many ways you can be use*ful*. It will make you a happier man, now, and when you have reached the other end of your life."

Anders nodded obediently. It was impossible to say if there was any agreement behind the obedience.

CHAPTER 17

Anders quickly learned to love the art of the gardener. It felt good to being doing something constructive with his hands. When he was not working, he enjoyed the company of his friends. He could want no better friends than Suzette and Elsa, and life was not so bad after all.

Suzette's mother sometimes sent her into town on errands. If his gardening work were finished, Anders might accompany her and bring Elsa as well. On one such occasion, they walked down the opposite side of the street from a horse cart parked before a storefront. In the cart, holding the reigns, sat a boy of 12 or 13. Behind, a man from the store loaded supplies into the bed, while the boy's mother supervised.

The boy, his mother, and the man loading supplies all took note of Suzette and Anders. "That's the Exchequer's daughter, isn't it?" the woman asked the man. "The one who nearly drowned beneath the ice last winter."

"And the young fellow who fished her out, I believe," the man answered.

"Ah yes, it must be," the woman remarked. "I wouldn't have recognized him. He's a university student, is he not?"

"*Was*," the man replied.

"Why do you say that?"

"He *was* a university student. Now, they say, he frolics around that big estate, playing children's games with the little girl."

The woman still watched Suzette and Anders. "They are between terms now, at the university, are they not?" she asked. "I suppose he'll be a university student again when the new term begins."

"I'm not so sure about that," the man said as he arranged sacks in the cart. "I heard he was let go from the university on account of his mental state. His professors are absolutely pulling out their hair over it. That's what I'm told, anyhow."

"Is it that bad?" the woman asked.

"It's not that he's a lunatic or anything like that. They just say it's kind of like he isn't all there anymore. Sort of what you might call a half-wit."

In the wagon, the boy perked up. He squinted to get a better look at Anders. He'd never seen a real, live half-wit before.

"That's odd," the lady commented to the man. "I'd heard he was one of the top students."

"*Was*," the man repeated. "Not since he went through the ice."

The boy in the wagon didn't hear this. He'd stopped listening and was instead focused on getting a better look at a full-grown half-wit.

"Such a tragedy," the woman sighed. "I was unaware it affected him so."

"Now he's no more fit for the university than that dog he walks with."

"That remark is beneath you, Mr. Kaat!" the woman protested, placing her hand over her bosom as if to protect her own heart from such denigrating words. "It's an unkind sling!"

The man bowed slightly. "Beg your pardon, ma'am. I was just repeating what I've heard from more than a few folks."

"Well, they shouldn't say such things either. They should take a moment to recall how he came to be this way. He deserves that much consideration at least."

"No doubt, you're right about that," the man agreed. "But, I guess people only think about what they see here and now, and don't recall much about what they might call *old news*."

"Well, they should make more effort to recall it," she insisted.

The man finished loading the wagon. "Yes, ma'am. They surely should. Will there be anything else then?"

"That's all, thank you," she said. The man nodded and went back inside the store. The woman climbed up beside the boy with the reins. The boy snapped the reins before she had seated herself, bringing her down with a thud. She swatted him. "Be careful, for Heaven's sake! Are you trying to kill me?"

"No, ma'am. Sorry," the boy told her without taking his eyes off the distant forms of Suzette and Anders. "I just wanted to catch up and get a good look at that half-wit."

"You just forget about that," the woman scolded. "You forget about all this half-wit talk altogether."

By the time they reached their home, the woman had taken her own advice. She had forgotten all about Suzette and Anders and the university and half-wits. The boy was a different story.

CHAPTER 18

As long as it was summer, Anders and Suzette were insensible to the things being said of him in the town. They were too busy enjoying simple pleasures to concern themselves with what others were doing or thinking. All too soon, summer came to an end, and young Suzette began her next year of schooling.

Anders and Elsa walked Suzette to her school every morning and returned to collect her at the close of the day. This being so, it did not take Anders long to notice that the other children looked at him with curious expressions. When Suzette came out of school to find Anders and Elsa waiting for her, she quickly guided them away from the other children. It didn't take Anders long to understand why.

The children gathered into little groups and whispered to each other as they watched Anders escort Suzette away. Anders could catch bits and pieces of their comments. "There he is. That's him," one boy said to his comrades. Another time, Anders heard one of them declare, "He's the one I told you about. He looks normal, but don't be fooled by that."

Anders knew their comments were the result of his fall from the intellectual pedestal within the lore of the community. He made every appearance of not hearing them. What good would it do to take issue with the whispered comments of school children when by opening his mouth, and showing the sluggishness of his speech, he would only add credence to their impressions of him? So he let them trade comments without raising a single eyebrow at what he heard.

Meeting no resistance to their gossip, some children became more bold. When the children burst forth from the school, one boy spied Anders waiting. He teased Suzette, "There's your half-wit boyfriend, come to take you home."

"That's a bold thing for you to say," Suzette yelled at the boy, "after the way you butchered your lesson today. *He* was chosen for the university. *You* will be lucky if the meat cutter will let a clumsy oaf like you apprentice in his shop."

The other children giggled at the boy. His face grew pink and he said no more. Suzette turned and walked away with Anders, perhaps believing she had put an end to the boy's mischief-making.

It was not to be so easy. The next day, one of the other boys took up the battle on behalf of the one Suzette had chastised. "There's your half-wit," this new boy teased. "Take him home and teach him his letters, why don't you?"

This boy was a better student than the previous one. Suzette did not waste any time belittling his scholarship. Instead, she threw down her things and ran directly at him. What he held in academic stature this boy lacked in physical size. Indeed, he was something of a runt, and so he ran away from Suzette, who was every bit as big as he was and a great deal more determined.

The other children gleefully made way for the pursuit. It was great sport to see if Suzette would catch the miscreant. It promised to be a good race, as the little pip was a slippery dodger and he had good cause to do his best to stay beyond the reach of Suzette's angry fists.

Just as the children were warming to the entertainment, Anders caught hold of Suzette. "Let me go! Let me go!" she cried. "I want to teach him a lesson!"

Anders held her tight. "Calm down," he said. "This is no way to behave."

"But I can't let them say such things! I can't let them make fun of you."

"Why not?" he asked. "Children must have their fun. What is it to me?"

She stopped struggling and looked into his face. "It doesn't bother you?" she asked.

He shifted his eyes away from hers for an instant. "No. It doesn't bother me at all." She let her fists unclench themselves and he let go of her. He went to where she had dropped her possessions and picked them up for her. The other children looked crestfallen at the sudden end to their entertainment, but they all remained silent as Suzette and Anders walked away.

The next afternoon, when the children were dismissed, little groups of them collected, waiting to see if anything interesting would develop. The boys who were at the core of the troublemaking stood together, whispering among themselves and casting expectant glances in the direction of Suzette and Anders. Suzette watched them as she walked to meet Anders, ready to reply to whatever taunts they might choose to throw at Anders with her words or her fists.

Anders focused his attention on Suzette, keeping the boys only in the background of his vision. He smiled at Suzette, just as he always did, showing no memory of the past days' troubles in his eyes. Maybe if he paid no attention to the boys, they would pay no attention to him.

The boys said nothing out loud while Suzette watched them. As she and Anders walked away, she cast glances over her shoulder. One glance caught a boy pointing at them and whispering some joke to his friends. Suzette stopped and marched back into the crowd of children. She turned her face from one end of the group to the other, so they would know what she was about to say was meant for all of them.

Suzette spoke in her loudest voice, that all might hear her. "I've had enough of this," she began. "I wouldn't think twice about chasing down and beating every single one who deserved it with my own fists. But that would embarrass my friend." She looked to where Anders and Elsa had stopped.

Turning her face back to the children, she continued. "Instead, I will introduce him to you, and see if your behavior changes once you know him." She motioned toward Anders. "This is my dear friend, Anders. He was the star pupil at the university." Her voice quavered a bit as she said the word *was*. "One day I had an accident and nearly drowned. I would certainly have drowned if he had not come to my rescue. He saved my life, and in doing so, almost drowned himself. Since then, he has been ill and has taken a break from his studies. That doesn't make him a half-wit. He is still smarter than all of you put together, and once his senses recover from his illness, everybody will see that."

She paused to steel herself for the challenge she was about to offer. "If anybody wants to call him names, this is your chance. It won't hurt him. He has faced far worse than your little sticks and stones. But if you want to make fun of him, do it in an orderly fashion, beginning with the most deserving." She looked from face to as she said her next words. "Who among you has saved another person's life at the peril of your own?" she asked. "Let him speak first."

The children searched each other's faces. The troublesome boys looked down, moving dirt around with their shoes. Suzette probed the eyes of the faces that would make contact with her, but no one had a comment to offer.

"I thought so," Suzette concluded. She walked to where Anders waited. They went away together.

They did not go directly home, for there was, in the town square, a beautiful fountain at which they liked to stop. They sat on the stone wall of the fountain and dipped their feet into the cool water. They remained silent, watching the goings on of the townsfolk for a while before Suzette finally spoke her mind. "You don't have to walk with me to school anymore, if you no longer wish it," she said.

"Why would I not wish it?"

"The boys," she said. "You pretend their words do not sting, but I know you too well. I can see in your face that it really does hurt you to be spoken of in the manner they do."

"You must not concern yourself with the boys. Their words mean nothing to me. And besides, I have an expert defender." He gave her a pat on the head.

"You say such things, and yet I can even now see the pain in your eyes. How am I to be happy when I know I am the bringer of that hurt to you?" Tears welled in her eyes, and if the truth be known, those tears hurt Anders far deeper than foolish taunts from schoolboys ever could. "They stayed quiet today," she went on through her tears, "but who knows what they will do tomorrow?"

The pain at seeing Suzette cry was like a white hot light searing its way through the center of Anders's heart. All at once it seemed as if the light had hit something hard within the core of his heart. It was as if there had been an explosion within Anders's chest, throwing off a firework of brilliant sparks, one or two of which soared so high as to reach his mind and reignite a fire that had once burned brightly there.

He threw one leg over the fountain wall so he could face her squarely. "You have brought me nothing but smiles. You are like the sweetest smelling rose in the garden. The only sadness that comes from you falls on those who must leave the garden." His gaze grew distant for a moment. Then it returned to her. A wonderful thing had happened. "I want to tell you something," he said. "I want to tell you a story."

Chapter 19

From where it came, he could not tell. It just came into him. It was as if he had been transported backward to the time when he sat at his father's knee. He could almost hear the words of a story flowing freely from his father's mouth. But these words flowed from his own mouth.

He spoke the story, and for the first time since his accident, he did not speak slowly or cast about for the right words. The words came to him readily, like when he was a boy entertaining his schoolmates with his tales. And the theme, and the characters, they came too. They came readily into his head. After nearly a year of having to think very hard to put every single thought together, the ideas washed over his mind like gentle waves and let their waters pour out through his mouth.

It was something that had not existed before, but it came into his head and he told it. Plain and simple in words and concept, it was a glorious leap for its creator. From beginning to end, it was a story, and that made all the difference in the world.

"A long time ago," began the storyteller, "there lived a wealthy king, who resided with his very beautiful daughter in a very grand castle. All around the castle they kept acres and acres of gardens, for they loved flowers more than almost anything else in the world.

"The king's daughter, the princess, who was to be married to a very handsome prince, loved roses best of all the flowers. 'At my wedding,' she declared, 'I will have great bouquets of roses picked from the gardens. But the sweetest smelling rose I will reserve for myself. I will wear it in my hair, and at the ceremony I will give it to my husband as a symbol of the sweetness of our love. It will have the place of highest honor among all gifts of affection,' she said.

"The roses overheard this talk, and it filled them all with dreams of glory. Soon they were all practicing smelling sweet, and trying to gain advantage over each other for the soft morning sunshine and cooling moisture from the earth. It was serious business, as the stakes were high.

"Now, in this garden there also lived a lowly earthworm. He was not pretty like the flowers, and he smelled of musty earth, but he was a good-hearted fellow. Every morning he passed by the roses on his way to his daily labors, and in the evening he returned home by the same route. But roses, you see, think quite highly of themselves and rather poorly of earthworms. Furthermore, they are not above letting anyone, especially earthworms, know their opinions. So every day, when the worm went off to work, the rose flowers made cruel jokes about his station in life."

"Where did he work?" interrupted Suzette.

"He worked under the earth, digging tunnels so that the rain water would drain properly to feed the roots of the plants in the garden. But the roses did not know this, because they had never cared to ask. Who cared what a worm did with his time? Therefore, they did not know the importance of the worm to their own success, and felt no guilt for teasing him."

"Were there no kind flowers?" Suzette asked.

"Now that you mention it, there was one kind rose flower that did not torment the poor worm. In fact, she spoke pleasantly to him, and asked after his wife and children. She alone, among all the roses, declared that the worm was her friend, and she wished him happiness.

"Of course, her friendship with the worm was not helpful in her relations with the other roses. They turned their noses up at her, as roses are wont to do. 'Well,' they said, 'she will certainly never adorn the princess's hair, for she lacks the proper society to be counted as a true rose.' Then they shook their heads that one of their own could sink so low and be such an embarrassment to them all.

"But she cared little for their opinions. She thought it would be a fine thing to be worn in the hair of the princess, but to her it was not worth the price of cruelty toward even the least of creatures.

"And so she continued, day after day, showing kindness to the lowly worm, thinking she was giving up her chance at becoming the highest symbol of love. But what neither she nor the other roses knew was that the worm was working at repaying her kindness. All the while, he was making sure the earth beneath her roots was tunneled and turned to her best advantage.

"Yet, even more important than that, was the advantage she gave to herself. You see, every time she showed kindness to the worm, her heart became sweeter. The sweetness of her heart made the pleasant odor of her petals the sweetest of all. And on the morning of the royal wedding, when the princess came to the garden to choose her special flower, it was but a short moment's work to find the sweetest smelling rose.

"At the ceremony, all the other roses watched as the princess gave her to the prince. The others were all soon thrown away, but she was carefully pressed and kept in a safe place, and the prince and princess looked upon her often, for she was a perfect symbol of the sweetness of their love."

Suzette's eyes widened with delight at the happy ending. "What a wonderful thing to happen!" she exclaimed. "But didn't the worm miss her terribly when she had gone?"

"Of course he missed her, but more powerful than the sadness of missing her was his joy for her happiness."

It was not the finest story ever told. Nor was it even the finest story Anders had ever told, yet it was a story, and that was certainly something. It was a welcome link to the days when Anders showed only promise. This tale had not the insight nor the depth of his best stories. It was far more elementary and lacked the elegance of that to which he had previously been able. It was naked in its simplicity when compared to the great half-masterpiece that lay collecting dust at the university. But it made Suzette feel better, and it provided Anders a glimpse of the past and a spark for the future.

When the story ended, the vision Anders had of his father faded. Though Anders struggled to hold it, it melted away into a dark corner of his mind. He tried to find it again, but he could see nothing in the darkness. It was gone, maybe for a while, maybe forever.

"That was such a wonderful story!" Suzette beamed delight at him. "Where did you hear it?"

Anders had to think hard to make sure he hadn't just overheard it from the gardener or someone else from his everyday life. When he was sure, he said, "I heard it from my father." He thought some more and added, "When I was a little boy."

Anders hadn't heard it from his father. He had only envisioned his father telling it to him. He had created it on his own. In some part of his mind he knew this, though he could not fully understand it, and certainly could not explain it to Suzette.

"Did your father tell you many stories?"

"Yes, he told me very many."

"Will you tell them to me?" Suzette pleaded. "I love stories."

Anders could not recall a single story his father had told him. He stammered. "Uh, well, I . . ." Then he found the confidence to say, "Yes. I will tell you all of them."

Even through this burst of confidence, both Anders and Suzette realized that Anders's speech had become slow and careful again, not easy and flowing as it had been when he was telling the story. Though they were each happy with the developments of the afternoon, they looked away from each other for just a moment.

Despite that one moment of disappointment, Anders was excited about what happened that day. Before he went to bed that night, Anders put the story down on paper as best he could remember having told it. In some places he could not remember exactly what he'd said, so he used different words. In other spots, he thought of a better way to say what he meant, so he substituted what he thought were finer phrases. At last it was all there, written in his inelegant penmanship. He studied the pages for some time and felt happier than he had in quite a long while.

Chapter 20

As time went by, Anders invented more stories for Suzette. When he worked in the gardens, he imagined that the plants, animals, tools, and whatever else he saw, had their own personalities. He thought of what they might say, and what they might do if they were like people.

This was hearty exercise for his mind, but his musings about the garden objects were disjointed bits and pieces. To arrange themselves into coherent stories, they needed a spark of inspiration. This spark was very difficult to control. It came, as it had the first time, without warning, bringing to Anders's mind the enticing vision of being a boy at his father's knee, hearing the words of the story from his father's mouth.

There was a kind of magic in this spark, for these were not the same stories Anders's father told him when he was a boy. These were new stories, created in that moment of inspiration. Anders could not have remembered those old stories so well, or spoken them so easily. But these fresh stories flowed from him gracefully. It was as though he became lost in them, and all the troubles of the world melted away. All his stumbling over ideas and words disappeared.

But even magic comes at a cost. For Anders the cost was a sort of frustration with his own mind. This magic spark of inspiration came when it would and went when it would. He could not hold onto it, which was the single thing he most yearned to do. It was like seeing the bright light of his own genius through the crack underneath a locked door. He longed to burst through the door and reclaim his light, but the door would not open for him. How tantalizing it was to see the light of inspiration within himself. How dispiriting it was never to be able to take hold of it.

When the light went away, Anders was left exactly as he had been since his accident. Slow and struggling of speech, he returned to the gardens and strained his mind to think deeper thoughts. But when the light was gone, his mind only bumped about in the dark, unable to improve itself.

In time, he made some progress. The spark was still fleeting. He could not grow it into a constant flame that would light up his whole mind as in former times, but he could bring it to himself more often. This meant he could tell more stories, even if he could do nothing else with the spark. At last, he could tell one of his little fairy stories nearly as often as he chose.

This progress mirrored the progress of his early youth. The more he controlled the frequency of the spark, the more the vision in it changed. Now, in his visions, he began telling the stories to his father. Just as he had taken charge of the storytelling in the old days, he was taking charge of it now. Finally, he became the sole storyteller in his visions. He gained the power to create a new story at will. Yet, when the story was over, he became the same quiet, slow Anders who had been pulled from a hole in the ice.

It became his routine to tell a story to Suzette when he and Elsa escorted her home from school. The three of them would stop and sit on the wall of the fountain, where he would tell Suzette a new story. Before long, the other girls from school began to gather at the fountain to hear the stories as well, as Anders's stories were ever so charming to young ears.

At length, all the girls were held captive by Anders's after-school stories. Since boys must know what the girls are about, they were soon brought in by their curiosity, only to fall under the spell of Anders's wonderful tales. None of the children called him names anymore, and those who had called him names before felt sorry for it.

It became a common sight in the town. On any school day, the stammering gardener of the Minister of the Exchequer could be seen at the fountain in the square, surrounded by scores of school children as he told his little fairy stories. The townspeople found no harm in it, just as they could see no particular benefit from it. It was nothing to them. But it was much to the children and Anders, so it continued day after day.

For more than a year the days passed in just this way. While the wide world turned about them, Anders, Elsa, Suzette, and Suzette's parents lived happily. Anders adopted a routine of gardening, telling stories, and playing games with Elsa and Suzette. Though it was not the life he had intended for himself, he was content. His pleasures were simple ones, but they were pleasures nonetheless.

Anders had not returned to the university. His professors, once so eager to have him back, had adopted new favorite students with whom to share their knowledge. If they ever thought of Anders, it was only to shake their heads and entertain a brief regret over what might have been. Then, they very sensibly returned their thoughts to their current students and the things that still might be.

In town, Anders's fame was completely different than it had once been. He was remembered as a hero dimly in the cobwebbed corners of the townspeople's minds. Now, he was merely that simple gardener man, who could be seen in the afternoon, telling silly little fables to the schoolchildren. He was a common fixture of the town square, like the fountain. There was nothing noteworthy about him, and he was hardly worth mention from one day to the next.

Anders was also a common sight within the house of the Minister of the Exchequer. Though his home was in the guest cottage, Anders was welcomed into the main house just as though he had been born into the family. He grew quite fond of both the Minister and his wife, and they came to love him as if he were their own son. Yet, in spite of the characteristics that sometimes made him seem younger, they never lost sight of the fact that he was now 18 years old.

This was the winter of Suzette's eleventh year. The family, and they all considered Anders a full part of it, sat at the supper table in the warm house while winter's cold reigned outside. It was something of an important supper, because next day the Minister would leave for his annual meeting with the heads of the Parliament. This was the last meal he would share with his family for a week or more.

"I shall have to do without a footman for my sled," Gustav told

70

his wife as he cut into his meat. "Poor Peter is ill with a fever." Peter was the Minister's footman. It was his place to ride on the back of the horse-drawn sled that would convey the Minister to the capital city.

"Can you manage without a footman?" his wife asked.

Gustav chuckled. "I could be very happy to live my whole life without a footman. But then, Peter is a good lad; he does very well. And then there are appearances. Everyone expects an official of the government to trail a footman behind him, and if he doesn't, it's practically a scandal. But there's nothing to be done about it. Peter is in no condition to travel, and it's too late to replace him."

"What are a footman's duties?" Anders asked.

The Minister smiled. "Oh, a footman's duties are very serious. You see, he must wear a general's uniform and stand up straight at all times. He must keep a stern look fastened to his face, and never smile, no matter how many silly old men of great importance parade before him. Oh yes," he continued, as if he had forgotten an inconsequential part, "and from time to time, he must carry a piece of baggage from one place to another."

Suzette giggled. "Papa, you simply cannot do without a footman then, for you are always laughing at the silly old men."

"Nonsense." The Minister assumed a comically exaggerated look of seriousness. "I shall look them all straight in the eye and scowl at each of them, just to make them feel more important."

"I'll do it!" Anders blurted out.

They all stared at him, attempting to place his words into the thread of their conversation. "Do what?" Gustav asked.

"I'll go as your footman."

"You?" Gustav asked. "It is very kind of you to offer, but I assure you, it is not necessary that I have a footman."

"But I want to do it," Anders protested.

"I have no doubt of it," the Minister reassured him. "But it is not a very comfortable ride, all day long uncovered on the back of the sleigh. It is cold and it may be wet. I would not put you through it."

"I want to do it," Anders repeated. "There's less for me to do here in winter." His eyes pleaded with Gustav. "I don't get to see many different places."

The Minister's wife took pity. "Gustav," she said, "wouldn't it be all right for him to go? It would be a treat for him to see Parliament. Keep in mind, those gossips at the Capital will make far more trouble of your lacking a footman than they will of your lacking a gardener."

"Do I care one whit about the gossips at the Capital?" Gustav scoffed. But he did care about the happiness of the young man who was almost a son to him. For this, he relented. "Very well, you will be my footman tomorrow," he told Anders. "We leave at sunup. You will have to go to the livery even earlier to be outfitted in your uniform. Take care to wear warm underclothes. It will be a long, cold journey."

Anders blushed at the mention of his underclothes in the presence of two females. But as his face was red, so were his teeth white, and everyone at the table could see them for his broad smile.

Chapter 21

Anders was waiting outside the livery when the stable boy came to open it up in the morning, notwithstanding the fact that a freezing rain was falling. Anders didn't think of the rain. He thought only that this was a chance to perform a service for the man who had given him a home and a family when he'd had neither. If there were any other thought dwelling in Anders's mind that morning, it was only of what a grand adventure it would be to travel to the most important place in the entire country.

The stable boy was not happy to learn that he would be required to help Anders assemble a proper uniform from among the footman's gear stored at the livery. After Anders showed his willingness to help the boy with his horses, the boy became rather more enthusiastic about outfitting him.

Anders thought the uniform they put together looked smart. The pantaloons and tunic were slightly large for his frame. Fortunately, he had heeded the Minister's advice and dressed himself in enough bulk of clothes to fill out the oversized pieces quite nicely. Altogether, he was very pleased with his new appearance.

While Anders and the stable boy worked at rigging the sleigh, the Minister's driver made his appearance. The driver was a gruff man, with a shaggy beard, bushy eyebrows, bloodshot eyes, and a large, red nose. He made no effort to help them. Rather, he made a sofa of straw and sat back with his hands behind his head.

Though the driver was wrapped up in a heavy coat and wore a fur cap, he shivered with cold. On occasion, he produced a flask from his pocket and took a long draw at it, muttering something about wanting to chase the chill out of his bones. Yet, each drink only seemed to make him shiver more. It must have been the shivering that made him surly. In between muttering to himself about the cold, he scolded the stable boy. "Mind those traces, boy!" he yelled out. "I don't want them tangled. I won't hesitate to box your ears if there's need of it."

The stable boy did not say anything. He merely kept at his work. Anders thought the boy knew his job very well, but that did not stop the driver from threatening to cuff him at every new task the boy undertook. Once, the boy rolled his eyes at Anders, but this was the only indication he was not focused only on his work.

They pulled the sled outside and hitched it to two fine horses. Anders went to the front of the house to serve the Minister. In another moment, Gustav emerged. Anders dutifully carried his baggage to the sleigh, where he secured it in its place.

The driver's demeanor was completely changed. In the presence of the Minister, he stood up straight and acted as if he had been active in preparing things for the journey. There was no sign of his flask.

"Good morning, Mr. Bleekner," the Minister said to the driver.

"A fine good morning to you, Mr. Minister." The driver removed his hat and bowed slightly. "Brisk day for a journey, sir."

"Brisk, and then some," the Minister replied. "I trust you have not over-fortified yourself against the cold. I need a sharp driver today."

"Oh no, sir," Bleekner insisted. "I'm bright-eyed as an owl and steady as an oak."

"Good. I needn't tell you how you earned a reputation that, I'm sorry to say, will hinder your employment as a driver. If not for my warm remembrance of your father, I'd give a long, second thought to employing you myself."

"Aye, I'm sure he sleeps more peaceful for your kindness to his boy." Bleekner held his hat in his hands in a sign of humble gratitude. But when the Minister turned away for an instant, the driver scowled contempt at him.

"I'm sure he'd counsel you to make the most of that kindness, Mr. Bleekner," the Minister said. "Be a sharp driver today. It would go a long way toward earning back your good name."

"Yes, sir. That's sound advice, sound advice, indeed." The driver smiled at the Minister, but to Anders it looked like his eye twitched a little bit as he did it.

Gustav turned toward Anders and the stable boy. "Everything set, Junius?" he asked the boy.

The stable boy nodded. "Rigged and ready, sir."

"Ready, Anders?" Gustav asked.

Anders hesitated. He wanted to warn the Minister that his driver was not as bright-eyed as he pretended. Over the Minister's shoulder, Anders could see the driver staring at him. The man bared his teeth as if he knew exactly what was on the tip of Anders's tongue and wished it known that it would be dangerous to utter the words.

"Anders?" Gustav repeated. "If you've changed your mind about going, it's not too late."

Anders shook himself, swallowing his warning. "No. I'm more determined than ever to ride with you."

Gustav took his seat in the sleigh. Anders found his place at the back, and the driver climbed up in front. The driver turned to face his passenger. "Begging your pardon, sir. Is it likely we'll be stopping by the inn at the Five Forks for a hot bite to eat?"

"We shall see what sort of time we make," the Minister replied. It would have been a very reasonable thing to say to a sharp driver.

The driver nodded and faced front. Anders heard the crack of leather on horseflesh and the sled lurched forward. Sitting backward, Anders watched the stable boy grow smaller as he fell away into the distance.

It had stopped raining and the sun was actually appearing over the horizon. The trip would not be a wet one, which was some comfort, but a cold breeze had come up from the North. The snow, which had been slushy, was now becoming hard and crusty. As they went along, the sleigh began sliding sideways a little when they went around turns in the road.

The morning sun can usually be looked to for warming rays to lessen the chill left by night. Today, the sun only made the cold wind blow colder. Anders tucked his hands under his arms to warm them. He brought them back out whenever the sideways sliding of the sleigh compelled him to use his hands to hang on so he was not thrown from the sled.

The icy road dictated that great caution should be used, but the freezing wind only seemed to make the driver want to go faster, in order to reach the inn in time to make a stop there. On a day like this, any man might look forward to the opportunity to go inside and be warmed by a hot meal, but the driver's urgency made Anders wonder if the inn might not be the place where the man hoped to replenish the dwindling liquid in his flask as well.

The way led over flat countryside at first. Presently, they began to encounter hills. The horses struggled pulling the sleigh up the hills on the icy road. The driver urged them on with the whip, yelling at them the entire time. Had the Minister not been sitting in the sleigh, it is likely the driver would have been even more harsh with them.

On the downslopes of the hills, the horses tread gingerly, using every instinct in their power to keep their feet under them. The driver had little patience for their caution. He did not care to delay getting out of the cold on account of the instinct of a couple of stupid beasts. Again, he urged them on to greater speeds than they wanted.

Anders felt the cold too, but still he wished the horses would be allowed to proceed at a slower rate, as their own wisdom dictated. But he was merely the footman. If the Minister said nothing to the driver, how did he have any right to protest? The Minister's head was bowed, covered by a thick, fur cap. Anders could not see his face at all. Perhaps he was asleep. Anders, sitting atop the baggage at the back, rather than being seated securely within the well of the sleigh, could not think of relaxing. He could do nothing but hold on tightly.

At last they came to the steepest hill yet. The driver stopped them at the base. He turned around and yelled to Anders. "You, footman. Step off. You're too much weight."

Anders got down without a word of protest. If it would help the horses in their struggle with the hill, he would gladly walk. As he turned to face forward, he found confirmation that the Minister was indeed asleep. The driver grinned as he looked back at the Minister. Following this, he reached into his pocket and pulled out his flask. "Here's to unwanted advice from uptight prigs who can't mind their own business," he toasted toward his unconscious passenger without a thought to the conscious footman. He took a long drink, draining the container.

Fortified with drink, the driver turned back to the horses. He used his whip with zeal to prod them forward. Even with Anders walking, they made slow progress. This displeased the driver and he showed his displeasure to the animals. Anders, feeling sorry for the poor beasts, put his shoulder to the sleigh and pushed.

Finally, they reached the crest. Anders waited permission from the driver to resume his seat. The driver never said a word. Instead, the sled began down the other side of the hill without waiting for him. Before he realized it, Anders had lost contact with the sleigh. He began to run, but he could not catch it. He yelled, "Wait! Wait!" but the driver did not seem to hear.

There was no hope of catching the sled going downhill. Though the horses wished to pick their way with care, the driver would not allow it. Anders fell farther and farther behind, as he couldn't run very swiftly on the slippery slope.

Halfway down the hill, the road veered to the left. Somehow, the horses managed to negotiate this turn, even at the speed to which they were driven. The sleigh could not follow the curve. It slid sideways, went off the edge of the road, and toppled over, rolling down the side of the hill.

Anders saw the driver leap from his seat, just as the sled turned over and toppled down the embankment. He could not see anything at all of Gustav.

CHAPTER 22

Anders crossed the icy road and plunged into the snow on the hillside. It was difficult to move quickly through the crusted snow, but Anders threw all his strength into reaching the bottom of the hill.

At first, a rise in the landscape before him prevented Anders from seeing anything at the bottom of the ravine. He could only see one of the horses; it had been torn from its harness as the sleigh overturned. The horse stood, dazed but unhurt, near the side of the road at the top of the ravine. Nearby was the dark form of the driver in the snow. There was no sign of Gustav.

As Anders topped the small rise and began his descent in earnest, he spied the sleigh below. It was turned on its side. The other horse, still hooked to its equipment, lay motionless beside it. Anders's eyes darted back and forth across the snow, but he could not find any form that might be the Minister.

Mere seconds had passed since the violence of the accident, yet everything seemed so still. Only Anders moved, stumbling through the snow, panting tired breaths. At last, tripping over his own feet with fatigue, Anders came down to the sled. The baggage at the back was still held in place where he had secured it. By the baggage alone, one might never have guessed the tumultuous journey the sleigh had just undertaken.

Passing around the corner of the sled, Anders found Gustav at last. Only his head and shoulders were visible, as the rest of him lay underneath the sled. Anders dropped to his knees. It was easy to tell that Gustav still breathed. His breaths were hard and raspy from the pressure on his chest. A trickle of blood flowed from the corner of his mouth. His eyes were closed.

Anders tried to rouse him, but without success. Panic seized the young man, but he quickly fought it off. Gustav was badly hurt, and panic would not save him.

Anders's first attempt was to lift the sleigh. He was not strong enough to flip it upright, but he could lift it off the injured man. Yet, he could not lift it and pull the Minister out from under it at the same time. He was loathe to set it down on the man again, but his tired arms would insist that he do it very soon, for he could not move it sideways the least bit.

Just as he was resigned to having to set it down again, the driver came stumbling near them. The driver stared at the Minister. His eyes grew with horror and his body froze in place.

"Pull him out!" Anders barked at the senseless driver. "Don't just stand there. Help me get him out!"

Under normal circumstances, Anders would never have thought to address the driver in this way, and the driver would never have suffered it. Now, the driver snapped out of his daze and did as Anders commanded without so much as a grunt. He tugged at the Minister's arms, dragging the man out just as Anders's strength abandoned him. The sled fell, but only on the hard earth.

Anders fell down beside Gustav. His arms and legs burned with pain from holding up the sleigh so long. But there was no time for pain. They must get Gustav to a doctor, and it must be done quickly. "How far ahead is the inn?" Anders asked the driver. "We must take him there."

The driver shook his head. "No. No," he sputtered. "He's as good as dead now." He reached inside his coat for his flask. "They'll blame me. It's that stable boy's fault, but they'll blame me." He put the flask to his lips and tilted his head far back, doomed to disappointment, for the flask was empty.

"Shut up!" Anders commanded. "Go get the horse from the top of the hill. Maybe we can get the sleigh back up to the road."

The driver tossed his useless flask to the side. "One horse? This ravine? Impossible!"

"Then the horse will carry him," Anders snapped back. "Go fetch it, now!"

Anders was relieved at how readily the driver obeyed. "They'll want my blood for this!" the man grumbled. But he went, and that was all that mattered to Anders.

While the driver was off collecting the horse, Anders did what he could to bundle up Gustav against the cold. His coat had come open and his hat was off. Anders fixed these deficiencies as best he could. As he pulled the coat around the Minister, Gustav's body flinched in pain and his breathing grew more labored. Anders loosened the coat, much relieved that this seemed to ease the unconscious man's distress.

Anders stood and looked over the top of the sleigh for the driver. The man had reached the horse. His attention was occupied by the leather straps about the horse's neck. This attention to unimportant details annoyed Anders. "Hurry!" Anders yelled at him. "There's no time to waste!"

The driver looked up at Anders, but he did not hurry. Instead, he used the straps to pull himself onto the horse's back. Once mounted, he turned and looked down the road in the direction they had been traveling. Anders wanted to yell at him to hurry again, but something made him understand that the words would be wasted. The driver looked back toward him, as if trying to settle his mind on something. Perhaps Anders should have looked away, but he did not think quickly enough. Instead, his eyes met those of the driver. That meeting was enough to settle the driver's mind. The man on the horse turned away. This time he turned the horse away too. Together, they disappeared down the road.

Anders stared after them. He couldn't believe a man was capable of such treachery. "Come back!" he shouted, but it was not a shout. It came out a whisper. His tongue understood that there was nothing to be gained by shouting. The driver was gone; no amount of shouting would bring him back.

Anders quelled the instinct to run after him. He had no hope of catching a mounted man, and every step in that wasted effort would take him further from Gustav. He must save his strength and his time. There was a long walk ahead of him and a heavy burden to carry.

Though Anders would give anything for five minutes of rest, five minutes might mean the difference between life and death. He knelt beside Gustav and pulled him up over his shoulder. But when Anders stood up, and the Minister's weight fell onto his shoulder, Gustav's body heaved with such pain that Anders quickly set him down. At this, Gustav settled himself into unconsciousness again.

It would not do to carry him. His insides could not take the strain. Anders looked about for something that would aid them. The horse still hitched to the sleigh was dead. The sleigh was an immovable wreck. The sides of it were badly dented and the wood of the flooring had broken away from the sides at the joint in long sections. Without the aid of several horses, there would be no retrieving the sleigh from the ravine. Even if it could be pulled out, it was doubtful it would stay in one piece.

Staring at the useless sleigh brought the full weight of Anders's predicament down on his shoulders. He stared mournfully at the gaps where the flooring had come apart from the sides. Those gaps were the very holes in his hopes. Then, all at once, through those same gaps came a ray of light.

Anders moved quickly once the idea took hold of him. He went around to what had been the top of the sleigh. Sitting on the side that was now on the ground, he kicked with all his might at the flooring. With every kick, the gaps widened. Finally, the flooring was almost completely separated from the sides. He went around again to the bottom of the sled and wrestled with the flooring until, at last, he was able to break it free from the rest of the sleigh.

The iron runners were still firmly attached to the flooring, but the seat had remained attached to the sides. Anders set the floor piece down on its runners. Now he had a much simpler sled, made up entirely of the floor of the original on its runners. Next, he took some straps from the harness of the dead horse and tied them around the front of the runners. That done, he gently lifted the Minister onto the platform he'd made.

81

He must find some means to keep the Minister from sliding off the sled. For this, he attacked the baggage. Shirtsleeves, trousers, whatever came to hand, he used to wrap around the Minister's arms and legs. Then he wound the other ends of the clothes around the bars connecting the platform to the runners and made them fast with knots. Satisfied he had constructed the best conveyance his materials would allow, Anders took his place at the front of the sled.

He knew it would take him a long time to pull the sled up to the road, if he were able to do it at all, so he began at once. He took hold of the straps he'd tied to the runners, looping them over his shoulders. Holding the ends of the straps against his chest with clenched fists, he began his ascent of the hill.

The runners were not meant for crusted snow. Anders made such poor headway that he doubted his ability to gain the road. At last, he noticed the snow had been packed down to some degree by the rolling down the hill of the sleigh. Anders made his way to this tragic path where the crust of the snow had been broken up. Here, he made better progress, though the slope still worked against him.

One tortured step at a time, Anders trudged up the hill. After each step he made his position secure, took a deep breath, and allowed the burning in his thighs to subside. Then came the next step, another deep breath, and more pain. Step after step, it was the same, and yet the top of the hill seemed no closer. Anders yearned to sit and rest, but there was no time. His progress was too slow as it was. He must not stop until help was found.

Finally, the top of the hill came within reach. Anders became impatient for his goal and stepped less carefully in his eagerness. His foot slipped. He fell onto his stomach, losing hold of one of the straps so that one side of his sled slid away from him. With his other hand he held desperately to the remaining strap. Now, face down in the snow, Anders clung to the one thin strap of leather that held the sled from tumbling down the hill sideways in a journey that would certainly mean the end of its weakened passenger.

For a moment, all was still. The sled waited to give itself up to the force of gravity should Anders falter in the slightest. Anders struggled to hold things steady as he took stock and determined what hope he had of recovering the situation. In that moment, a memory thrust itself into Anders's mind.

It was the vision of a struggle against the winter elements. He saw himself calling up every ounce of strength in him to lift a little girl onto the ice. He had battled cold, dark, weariness, and pain, and he had succeeded in bringing the girl to safety. He had succeeded because he had been meant to succeed, and he was meant to succeed now. This trial could be no more difficult than that old one had been. It was only necessary to remember he was meant to succeed. So long as he never gave up that one thought, nothing was lost.

With his free hand, Anders rolled himself onto his back. Then he took hold of the remaining strap with both hands. It would be no easy task to pull the sled up to him now that he could not pull it straight on its runners. Nonetheless, it must be done, and in this he was meant to succeed.

The sled skidded sideways toward him slowly. It made only a small bit of progress before the runner became held up on something. He could pull it no further. He must straighten the sled before he could pull it up the hill. Very well, then that is what he would do. Hand over hand, he worked his way down the strap, holding the sled in place as he pulled himself down to it. It was slow work, but at last he came close enough to recapture the second strap.

With both straps in hand, he was able to tug the sled around and make it point toward himself again. But now he dare not try to turn around and regain his feet. Still, the manner of his success meant nothing to him, so long as it was success. Sitting in the snow, facing his sled, was not the best position from which to make progress up the hill, but progress was not impossible.

Anders hopped himself back a little ways, dug in his feet, and pulled the sled up an equal distance. This he did again and again. A half-step at a time he scooted himself, and then the sled, up the hill. It may have taken him minutes to reach the road, or it may have taken him hours; he was insensible to time. Time was crucial, and yet it was secondary. What mattered most was that he succeed, and he did succeed, because a memory told him he must.

With himself and his sled safely on the road, Anders lay back and panted refreshing air into his exhausted lungs. It would have been natural and easy for him to lie there for a long time to recover himself after the labor he had performed. But now the importance of time returned to his mind. Rest must wait until his success was complete, and it was still far from complete.

Anders climbed back to his feet, ready to take the next step toward help. But in which direction should that step be? He hesitated. There was an inn ahead on the road, but he knew not how far ahead. Home was, under the current circumstances, hours and hours away in the other direction. The inn might be just around the next bend in the road. Yet, it could just as easily be hours away as well.

Judging from how far they had travelled already, Anders guessed the inn was closer. He was turning in that direction when another thought struck him. At home, a doctor could be fetched quickly. What were the chances a doctor would be on hand at the inn? Someone from the inn would need seek a doctor. There was no telling how far they must go to find one, or what transportation they would have to take them. Anders knew where home was, and he knew a doctor could be found there. He turned in the direction of home.

It was now afternoon. Darkness would fall before they reached home. This was unavoidable, yet it was important that Anders reach the flat land with his cargo before night. It would be a great danger to try and navigate these icy hills in darkness. He cast aside all thoughts of rest and bent his weary body toward the immense task at hand.

It was good fortune that he had already topped the steepest hill. Yet, travelling down that hill would be no easy journey. The difficulty lay in holding the sled back, for it wanted to go down the hill at a rate that, left unchecked, would certainly send it careening off the side of the road again. Anders struggled to hold the sled back. The footing was poor, but to lose his footing meant being dragged down the hill until some tragedy brought an end to the sled's travels.

At last, the bottom of the hill was safely gained. Anders felt as used up as if he had dragged the sled up the hill, so fiercely had his muscles strained to keep control of it. His legs, arms, and back burned with pain. Every instinct told him to drop to the ground and rest his aching body. But there was another hill ahead of him, and the day was growing old. He fought off the desires of nature, and put one foot forward toward the next hill. His other foot obediently followed.

The remaining hills were less steep, which is the only reason Anders was able to conquer them. Step by step, he pulled his burden behind him. At length, the agonizing pain in his body was replaced with a sort of numbness. He recalled this numbness. It was the same he had felt when he had struggled to keep his head above the icy water those years ago. It was a kind of darkness, beckoning him. It enticed him with the promise of an easing of pain, for his body as well as his mind. It seemed to offer mercy from the cold world and from a hard life.

But there is no mercy in darkness. It is a lie. Anders knew this. He knew this not because he had any special wisdom. He knew this because he could see in the darkness the outline of a door, shown by the light that escaped through the cracks around it. This was the light he saw whenever a miracle in the form a story came into his head. It was the light that inspired him to pass through the darkness, for there was something more on the other side of it, if only he could persevere long enough to reach it.

This light alone kept him from falling down and freezing into the road. He set his sights on the light peeking out from under that door. Did he get closer with every step? He didn't know. As long as there was light under the door, there must be light behind it. Would he ever reach it? Maybe not. Certainly not, if he surrendered to the darkness.

One foot stepped past the other.

Night was beginning to fall, with still many hours of hard travel ahead. If there were some little thing in which to take consolation, it was that Anders had put the hilly part of his journey behind him. Now there was a vast flatness ahead, though even this would be difficult to pass in the dark, especially because Anders had used so much of his strength overcoming the hills.

Gustav had begun to issue strange noises from his throat. Mixed with these were labored coughs. While there was still a little light left in the day, Anders put down his harness straps and went back to see if there were some way he could improve Gustav's comfort. At once he noticed the poor man producing blood in his mouth with each cough.

Using some of the extraneous bit of clothing with which the man was secured to the sled, Anders cleaned out the blood as best he could. Then, he turned Gustav's head as much to the side as was practical, in order that the fluid did not clog his throat. Anders did not know what it was that made the man cough, but against the chance that it was the cold, he took off his fancy footman's coat and lay it over the Minister. With all this done, Anders's skill at nursing was exhausted. There was nothing left but to return to his place and resume his march.

Anders did not miss his coat for some time. He had been working hard all day, perspiring rather than shivering. But as the night wore on, and the temperature fell, his perspiration of the afternoon began to freeze to him, making the cold all the more bitter. Still, as long as there were strength left in him, he was determined to go on. In the dark of night, he could see the light spilling out from under his mind's door. He shuffled toward that light.

Since noticing Gustav cough blood, Anders had redoubled his efforts. This reaction was quite natural; it was also unwise. The extra exertion, combined with the growing cold, exacted a heavy toll from Anders's body. Worse was the burden to his spirit.

He shuffled one foot past the other. Then, again, the other foot. Then, he did nothing. He had meant to shuffle the first foot forward, but it did not move. He tried again, but it would not go. He knew he must concentrate harder on the light. But now that light was dimming.

Anders struggled to thrust forward both his body and his vision, but his feet were immovable. He focused his vision, but the lights at the sides of the door were gone. The light beneath the door receded from the ends toward the middle, growing shorter as he watched.

His legs buckled. He fell to his knees. The light narrowed to a point in the middle. He dropped his leather traces. The light was small now. He fell forward. His head lying on the icy road, he looked for the light. It was only a pin prick in the distance. It was a tiny speck, but he would hold it in his mind to the very last moment. It was his light. It was himself.

The light was all but gone now. In the next moment, it would surely be extinguished. When it was gone, Anders would never rise again. Gustav would expire where he lay on the sled. Tomorrow, they would both be found frozen to the road. Anders had done all he could to reach the light, but the light would not allow itself to be reached.

Anders let his eyes close. A moment later, he tried to open them again and was surprised to learn that he could do it. He was even more surprised to see that the light had not disappeared. It was still there, a speck in the vast dark distance. What was it waiting for? He had given all he had to give, and failed. Why did the light not just go out and put an end to his misery?

But the light did not go out. To Anders's amazement, it seemed to be very slowly growing brighter. It did not spread itself out in both directions like a light under a door. Instead, the dot stayed as a dot, but it became brighter. For a long time, Anders did all he still owned the power to do; he watched the light.

After some time, he heard faint noises. He could not identify the noises, but they were coming nearer. They were not human noises; this much was plain. Beyond that, the only thing Anders could tell about them was that they grew louder just as the light grew brighter.

The growing light and sound meant someone or something was

approaching. What light and what sound would come out of such a cold, inky blackness? "Is this The Reaper, coming to claim my soul?" he wondered. "If so, he must have it, for I cannot keep it from him."

At last the sound allowed some definition. Anders discerned the noise of horses plodding over the ice, mixed with the sound of iron runners sliding over the road. The light could now be seen to swing from side to side in an arc. This was a sleigh, with a lantern hung at the front.

The noise grew so loud Anders feared the horse and sleigh would run right over him. Before that could happen, there came the first human sound. "Whoa!" shouted a husky voice. "Whoa there!" The sound of the horses and sleigh diminished to nothing. The figure of a man emerged from behind the light.

The man came forward and made surprised exclamations as he surveyed the unlikely scene in the road before him. He was quick to action, and soon had helped Anders to his feet. Anders, realizing this was not The Reaper, but merely another hardy traveler, made what explanations he could, though his condition forbade him from saying very much.

The man did not need to hear the details. His eyes told him all he needed to know of the distress upon which he had come. He went to work at once putting Anders into his own sleigh. In the next moment, he had turned his sleigh around, so that it was facing in the direction from which he had come.

There was no room in his sleigh to allow the Minister to lie prone, so the man quickly made the decision to hitch the makeshift sled Anders had fashioned to the back of his own sleigh. Thereby, Gustav would not be squeezed into a dangerous position within his crowded conveyance. When all was ready, the man said a word to his horses. They started, making the journey at the fastest pace prudence would allow.

CHAPTER 23

They reached home as the dawn's first light was chasing darkness from the eastern sky. The entire house was roused from its slumber in an instant. The Minister was gently carried to his bed, and no fewer than three servants were dispatched to fetch doctors.

Anders, half frozen and exhausted, saw the Minister safely into the hands of his people before allowing the strain of the past day to overcome him. Soon, he was spirited away to his own sick bed. There, renewed warmth replaced the numbness of his body with the deferred weariness born of his toils. His muscles ached and his mind was used up, but there was no injury a good rest could not mend.

Anders slept through the day. His sleep was deep and dreamless, so that when he finally did awake, his mind was a clean slate. The first thing he saw was Elsa's loving face, where she had come around to the side of the bed to investigate the rustling noises he made. This was quite a pleasing sight. It was just such a welcome to the world of the awake as Anders might receive on any normal morning.

But this was not morning; this was late evening, and Anders was not in his own bed. The room was one within the main house. In the corner chair slept one of the household servants, head slumped over to the side in peaceful repose. Waking up here seemed strange, and this strangeness began filling the slate of Anders's mind with images of the recent past.

Anders sat up with a start. He threw the blankets off and slid out of bed. A quick search of the room rewarded him with some house clothes. He threw on these garments. Without waking his attendant, he slipped out of the room.

The house was all lit up, but it was as quiet as a tomb. This house did not sleep tonight, but in wakefulness it was afraid to make a noise. Bright light and silence are an unnatural pair in the night. Together, they bode ill for a household. A house lit so brightly at night should be filled with festive noise. This house's silence told its story. The cold silence made Anders shiver.

Anders crossed the balcony above the main staircase. Below, the main hall was flooded with light, yet not a soul was to be seen. Light wards off the night. Prayers are said quietly in private.

Beyond the head of the stairs, Anders entered the family's wing of apartments. Normally, he might have felt uneasy about trespassing within such a private area. Tonight, uneasiness did not turn him back. It drove him onward.

The door to the Minister's suite was ajar. Anders, with Elsa at his heel, stopped short of the doorway. He paused to take a deep breath before peering through the opening. In the Minister's sitting room, Suzette and her mother sat together on a sofa. Suzette leaned her head against her mother's bosom. Her mother held the girl firmly in her arms. Neither spoke.

Anders felt a tinge of embarrassment when Suzette's mother saw him in the doorway, but he made no attempt to hide himself. She motioned for him to sit with them. He obeyed without hesitation.

Suzette attempted to smile at him, but there were too many tears in her eyes. With Elsa at their feet, they sat together in silence.

The door to Gustav's bed chamber was closed. His wife and his daughter looked anxiously at it every few moments. Either happiness or tears were forming behind that door. In good time, it would open, and whichever had won the day behind it would rush out over them all and carry them where it would. Their eyes moved to the door and then back again.

For a long time they waited in silence. At last, the door opened. They all held their breath as the doctor came out. He looked worn and haggard, as if he had been working for a long time without rest. He stopped after taking one step into the room, looking sympathy at them through his bloodshot eyes.

The doctor signaled Suzette's mother to come into the bedroom. She rose and followed him, Suzette clinging tightly to her side. Anders wished very much to go in with them, yet he sat still, allowing them the privacy of their family. He kept to the waiting place of a trusted friend and loyal servant.

After a while, the door opened again and Suzette came out. Tears flowed down her cheeks. She walked slowly to Anders and spoke words so soft he could barely hear. "Papa wishes to speak to you," she sobbed.

Anders took her hand and they entered the bedroom. Gustav's eyes were open, but his face was drawn and pale. He breathed shallow breaths, punctuated by regular, weak coughs.

Suzette led Anders to the bed, where her mother gently stroked Gustav's hair. Gustav did not see Anders until the young man was quite near the bed. Then, recognition overtook the injured man's face. He struggled to speak. "Anders," he whispered. "You saved me once." Gustav's eyes moved to Suzette then came back to Anders. "And you would have saved me again. But it was not God's will this time."

Anders shook his head in protest at this statement. Gustav paused to cough, then went on. "I know all you did. I saw your strength, and your devotion." A cough interrupted him again. "I can't begin to repay you for your service to this family. Only allow me to grow my debt to you even deeper by letting me, this once, call you Son."

To have a man such as Gustav speak this way of him was a high honor, yet something within Anders rebelled against it. Tears flowed from his eyes as he spoke. "I don't deserve to be called your son. Your son would be no coward."

Everyone looked at Anders with an expression of shock.

"I could have saved you," Anders continued. "It required only the courage to move my tongue. I should have warned you. The driver had been drinking from his flask all morning. I should have told you he was drunk, but I was afraid. I was afraid of what he would do to me if I spoke the truth. This is what has come of my cowardice." He fixed his eyes on Gustav's battered form.

Gustav used all of his strength to shake his tired head. "No," he whispered as forcefully as he could. "It is my own fault. I knew his reputation. I wanted to give him a chance to redeem himself, even if I suspected he could not do it. It is I who put you in danger, and for that I am truly sorry."

"You made a mistake out of generosity," Anders insisted. "I made a mistake out of fear. The mistake of cowardice is harder to forgive."

Gustav strained to make himself understood. "*I* was in charge," he said. "A safe journey was *my* responsibility. You have long since proved you are no coward. And you are far too wise to believe in an idea that has been proved false. Carry this burden of undeserved guilt no further. It will bring you no good. I beg you, lay it down, here and now."

Anders nodded. Whatever the thoughts in his mind, this was the only answer he had the heart to give. No words found their way to his mouth. Tears rolled down his cheeks. The look in Gustav's eye said he was satisfied with this.

At this, all fell silent. The only sound was that of Gustav's breaths growing shallower. There was peacefulness on his face, which he tried with his eyes to cast about his family. But those eyes faded with his breath. Gustav's loved ones counted every second until his eyes closed and his breathing rattled to a stop.

Then they stopped counting; the seconds had lost their meaning.

CHAPTER 24

A man of the Minister's standing cannot leave this world without a certain amount of ceremony. A nation of people came forth, rich and poor, famed and unknown, to pay their respects. Then came the grand funeral a man so vital to the machinery of the state must produce at his passing. To the man who was gone, all this display meant nothing; to his family, it was yet another weight laid atop their mourning hearts.

Suzette and her mother bore this weight with uncommon grace, owing more to the character of each, than to their positions in society. Though their hearts were breaking, they made themselves presentable at every place and time where their presence might be expected. Though they only wanted to think of their beloved father and husband, they greeted well-wishers and replied graciously to every expression of sympathy. Holding their grief at bay, they stood in the public eye, showing their love and respect for the man they had lost.

Anders did all he could for them, while keeping out of sight as much as possible. He might have been thought a hero for all he'd done to rescue the Minister, but it is difficult to find a hero in an ending that does not turn out so happily. This suited Anders. He had been a hero once before, and he wished no more of it, especially since he thought of his role in the accident as less than heroic. He was quite satisfied that his efforts to save the Minister were of little interest to the people. They flocked to Suzette and her mother. Anders was content to stand behind and help them stand up to the flocking.

At last, the Minister was buried and the estate became quiet again. Everyone resumed their normal lives as best they could under the new circumstances.

Suzette fell into long periods of thoughtfulness. Anders suffered his own quiet moments of reflection as he struggled with the memory of how a word from him might have averted the tragedy of Gustav's death. Yes, Gustav had absolved him of responsibility, but he had not absolved himself.

In the gray days between winter and spring, Anders, Suzette, and Elsa walked together through the gardens. Snow, then mud, forbade outdoor games, but no one was quite ready for games anyway. There was still too much remembering the past and envisioning the future taking place, making their minds too heavy for play.

One day as they walked together, Suzette broke a long silence. "Do you believe in Heaven, Anders?"

"Yes," he replied. Then he added, "I think so."

"You're not sure?"

"No. Not really," he admitted. "I think souls go somewhere. I'm just not sure where."

She looked at the sky. "Do you think Papa is looking down over me? Watching over me?"

"I think he's with you and your mother in one way or another."

"I think so too, but how can I be sure?"

"I don't know if you can be. It's just a feeling you get."

"Do you get that feeling with . . ." She hesitated over broaching a topic of which he rarely spoke. "With your parents?"

"Yes. I do."

"Tell me about it," she begged. "Tell me what happened to your parents and how you feel them with you."

He told her the story of how he had lost his parents within a short time of one another.

"I don't know if I could live through losing *both* my parents like that," she told him when his story was over. "Tell me about how you feel them with you. Sometimes, I feel that Papa is still with me, but then I think I'm just being a silly little girl and he's really parted from me forever. I want to know he's really there."

"Sometimes, when I'm telling a story," Anders began, "it feels like I'm a little boy again, sitting at my father's knee. I hear him telling me a story. Or, sometimes, I hear myself telling him a story."

"And it's not just a memory?" she asked.

"No. It's like there's a room in my head and he comes to me

94

there. We meet and we say things we've never said before. We make new stories together. I can only do it when he's there."

"Does your mother come too?"

"No. I feel her presence there, but I don't see her."

"Do you ever see her?"

"Yes. Sometimes."

"Where?"

He hesitated. "Promise you won't laugh."

"Why would I laugh?"

"Because it may sound foolish."

"I'm sure it won't."

"Well, then I'll tell you." He paused, still unsure of himself. "Sometimes I think I see my mother in Elsa's gentle eyes. In the way Elsa keeps guard over me, and always makes sure I feel loved."

Elsa cast him a glance each time he said her name, but otherwise did not alter her gait as they walked.

"Do you think Elsa has the spirit of your mother?"

"I think Elsa is a regular dog," he replied. "But sometimes I feel like my mother's spirit uses her to watch over me. Does that sound foolish?"

"I guess not." The words were quiet and choked, as if the speaker were trying to hold back sobs.

Anders took her by the arm. "Suzette, what is it? What's the matter?"

She looked up into his face. This time the sobs could not be held back. "At least you feel her somewhere. With every day that passes, I worry that Papa is farther and farther away from me. I want to believe he's still here with me in some little way, but I can't trust that it's not just wishful thinking."

Anders knelt and gave her a hug. "It's all right, Suzette. Only, maybe you shouldn't look so hard. Think about the best times you had with him. His spirit will be in the memories. I'm sure of it."

"I try to," she replied, holding tightly to Anders. "I try to, but all I can see is the memory of him in that bed, the last night. I can only see his face, so drawn and pale, not at all like he really was. Sometimes I think I've forgotten what he really looked like. I can't see his true face in my mind."

Anders pulled back from her and looked into her eyes. "Maybe I can help you remember," he said.

For a moment, her eyes found their luster. "I would love it if you could!" Her eyes dimmed. "But how?"

"First things first," he said. "Let's get out of the cold. A warm mind remembers best."

They were near his cottage. He led her inside and made them both something hot to drink. They sat with Elsa in front of the fire. "Now that we are comfortable," Anders said, "I'd like to tell you a story."

Chapter 25

Suzette had been hoping for some great secret for remembering. She loved Anders's stories, but they were for fun, not serious matters. "Oh, Anders," she sighed, "I don't know what your talking roses can do. They can't bring Papa back. What good are they now? Nothing in the world can bring him back. What good is anything now?"

"This isn't a story about talking flowers," he assured her. "It hurts me to see you this way. Stories are all I have to ease your pain. Please, let me try to help."

"All right," she said. "Tell me a story. Do anything that will make it not hurt so much."

Anders had not thought up the story he would tell until this very moment. As he opened his mouth to speak, his mind raced backward in time to his childhood. There, in the house of his birth, at the knee of his father, was the perfect place for stories to be born. There, in the bright light that shone beneath a door in a dark corner, this story was born unto his mind. He spoke it as quickly as the light brought it to him.

"In one of the warm countries, near the sea, lived a boy named Carlo. He and his parents shared a little cottage some distance from a beach of smooth, white sands. They did not have much, but they had enough to live. They had a roof, clothes to shield themselves from the hot sun, and enough food to keep hunger from their door. Besides this, they had love for one another, which is a significant thing to have, especially when one is poor.

"Carlo's parents could not afford much beyond the necessities of life. They made up for this through the power of their own invention. They made up games to play with him, so that he played with them as happily as he played with other children. His father crafted toys for him out of driftwood and seashells, and whatever other useful objects he could find washed up on the beach.

"Carlo and his father particularly liked to go to the beach. It was a

97

wonderful place to race about in bare feet. The sand was perfect for molding into the shapes of all the artful things their minds conceived. And then there was the joy of discovering what relics the sea might throw onto the edge of land from its store of treasures. Whenever they had time to spend together, Carlo and his father could be found at the beach.

"They did not have all the time they would like to play together, for Carlo's father must work hard to keep a roof and a table for his family. He worked upon the ships that plied the sea all about. When he was gone to work, he was missed dearly, but when he returned, there was extra love, stored up for him from his little family.

"One day, Carlo's father did not come back. He had been claimed by the very sea he loved so much. Just as the sea gives up treasure, it sometimes takes treasure from us, and though Carlo and his mother might cry a million tears, the sea would not ever give back their most precious treasure.

"Carlo and his mother were strong, hard-working people. It was a great burden, but they found a way to keep themselves, month after month. And as the months passed, they used their constant toil to push the sadness away. But the sadness was clever, and it found the means to assail them when they were off their guard.

"Whenever sadness caught hold of Carlo, he went to the beach to look out over the sea. Sometimes he saw ships on the horizon, and he imagined that one of these ships was bringing his father home to him. He would hold onto this lovely thought until the ship passed from view. Then the thought would float away into the sky and wait for the next distant ship.

"One day while Carlo sat on the beach, letting his thoughts drift between the ships and the clouds, he began to cry. It had become too difficult to keep imagining that the next ship would bring his father home. Sadness penetrated the barrier of his imagination and swept down over him with more force than ever. No matter how he tried, he could not stop crying.

"All at once, a warm breeze swept over him. Though the breeze was warm, it made him shiver. He opened his eyes and realized he had cried himself to sleep in the sand. Some impulse made Carlo look into the breeze, for it did not seem the normal sea breeze to which he had grown accustomed.

"He saw nothing unusual in the breeze, but he felt it whisper into his ears. 'Look what love has grown for you,' the breeze whispered. At the same time, the breeze, as though it possessed tender hands, gently turned Carlo's head toward the beach beside him. Here he saw an unusual thing that had certainly not been there when he fell asleep.

"Carlo rose and walked toward the new object. It was a tiny tree, growing up from the sand. The tree was not as tall as Carlo himself, but it had as many branches as any tree of normal size. Among all of these branches, not a leaf was to be found. Indeed, all of the branches, save one, were barren, and came to a point like the boney fingers of a skeleton.

"The branch that was the exception was barren as all the rest, except at the very tip, where a seashell hung like the colorful bud of a flower. The outside of the shell was swirled with beautiful shades of blue. The inside was a smoothly polished mother-of-pearl.

"The voice of the breeze had told Carlo that this had been put here for him, so he was bold and plucked the shell from the branch. Now, the first thing a boy does when he picks up a seashell is to put it to his ear. Carlo was quite normal in this regard. He listened for the sea, but the sounds he heard were not sounds of the sea.

"What Carlo heard in the shell was laughter. It was the laughter of a child, blended ever so harmoniously with the laughter of a man. It was the echo of his own laughter as well as that of his father. He knew this in an instant. And he knew the exact time and place when that laughter was first heard.

"It was from a time when Carlo was just a very little boy. His father had been chasing him around the outside of their cottage. 'You can't catch me!' the boy yelled as he ran and giggled. The man made a show of almost catching hold of his little one, but somehow the boy always slipped through his grasp. And at each narrow escape, they both laughed all the louder.

"The sounds from the shell made Carlo see this distant day in his memory. He had not remembered this day in a very long time, and the rediscovery of it made him smile as he had not smiled since his father was lost. As long as he held the shell to his ear, he was happy again, as he had not been in a long while.

"At last, the sound of laughter from inside the shell faded away. Carlo took it from his ear. The sun was sinking low, and he still had chores to do, so he turned away from the sea and took his new shell home.

"Carlo felt better for a little while, but after a few days, he began to feel very sad about missing his father again. As was his wont, he went to the sea and sat on the sand. The little tree from which he had plucked the shell was gone, so he let his thoughts drift among the clouds.

"All at once, the warm breeze stirred him. He had been sleeping again. He looked out over the sea and heard the whisper of the breeze once more. 'Look what love has grown for you,' the breeze repeated. Carlo turned his head. The little tree had returned.

"This time there were two shells on the tree. The one Carlo had plucked before had been replaced by an identical shell. At the end of a different branch was another shell, this one hued in shades of gold.

"Naturally, Carlo wished to try a new color. He picked the golden shell and placed it next to his ear. In this shell he heard the sounds of tools being worked upon wood and the familiar voice of a man giving instruction.

"Carlo remembered these sounds. They came from the time when his father taught him how to fashion useful items from the driftwood they found on the beach. Carlo's memory followed the sounds. They stood together by the workbench. His father showed him how to plane the wood to make it straight. Next, they cut the pieces to the right size, before fastening them together and finishing the smooth surfaces. They made a small chest for Carlo. He had, ever since, kept it in a safe place and used it to hold his prized possessions. But what he prized most of all was that he had made it together with his father.

"After a while, the sounds of the woodworking faded away. The day was fast growing into evening. Carlo took this new shell and went home to his mother.

"Carlo put both his shells into the chest he'd made with his father, on top of his other belongings, to show they were first among all his keepsakes. He closed the lid and put the box away, but the memories the shells brought were always kept fresh in his heart.

"The days passed, and every time Carlo fell to sadness at missing his father, he visited the beach to seek the shell tree. He could never find it at first, so he would sit on the sand and think of the shells he had already gathered and the memories they brought.

"At length, a warm breeze would rush over him and let him know he had fallen asleep. Then he would hear the breeze saying to him, 'Look what love has grown for you.' He would turn and see the shell tree again, and it would have a shell of a new color to go with the shells he had already plucked from its branches.

"Carlo would pick up each new shell and hold it to his ear. From the shell would come the sounds of a memory. Each memory was of a time he had shared with his father. Carlo would listen, and remember, until the sounds from the shell faded. Then he would go home and carefully add the new shell to his collection in the box he had made with his father.

"At last, there came the time when Carlo's box was packed full of shells. He had taken all of the other things out, but even with only shells inside, the box was full to the point that nothing more would fit. Added to his first shells of blue and gold were shells of many other hues. There were reds and greens, grays and purples. The shells were so finely polished that all the colors within the box seemed to run together into a beautiful shining ray of light, so that it was impossible to tell one shell from another without taking it out and examining it closely.

"The next time Carlo went to the beach, he was wakened by the warm breeze, the same as always. The voice of the breeze said to him, 'See what love has grown for you.' Carlo looked, but this time there was no shell tree.

"He ran to the spot where the tree should have been, but there was nothing but empty sand. Carlo kneeled down and searched with his hands. He moved the sand from side to side, but there was no trace of his tree to be found. Carlo felt tears coming to his eyes.

"The warm breeze came over him again. The voice of the breeze spoke to him once more. 'The shells of the tree are mere tools,' the voice said. 'They have helped you to remember. Now your memories are kept safe in your heart. Hold them there always and cherish them. They are truly what love has grown for you.' Then the voice faded and the breeze blew out to sea.

"Carlo held his tears, for the voice was right. He had so many wonderful memories of his father in his heart, where they would live with him always. He no longer needed anything to help remind him.

"He went home and opened his special box. He was not surprised to find it empty. The shimmering shells were gone. But one beautiful shining ray of light still beamed forth at him from the box that he had built with his father.

"Carlo kept the box empty for the rest of his days. But whenever he opened it, a shining ray of light beamed out at him. It was the same shining ray of light that glowed around his heart. And it shone there always, always."

When Anders had finished, Suzette threw her arms around him and hugged him with all her might. "Oh, Anders," she cried, "do you think I shall ever have a shell tree for my Papa?"

"I know you will," he said. "We shall make one. We will make a shell for each memory."

"Can we? Can we start now?" She pulled her head back from him to look at his face. Through her tears came the first faint trace of a smile. It was her first smile in ever so long.

They made a shell tree for Suzette out of papier-mâché. Suzette made a shell to represent every cherished memory of her father and hung each of them with string from the branches of the tree. Whenever she began to feel sad at missing her father, she would take down one of her shells and blend its bright light with the bright light within her heart. The memories made her smile and allowed her to recall her father's face as it truly was. It always made her feel better.

Her shell tree, together with her mother's love, and her friendship with Anders and Elsa helped her overcome her grief at losing her father. As time passed, she began to play games with Anders and Elsa again. She went back to school and became a normal girl once more.

CHAPTER 26

As Suzette mastered her grief, time passed. Before anyone knew it, five years had gone by. Suzette was a beautiful young woman of 16, ready to leave childhood behind and set out into the world as an adult.

Time brought other changes as well. Now, Suzette helped her mother manage the estate, no easy task considering the vastness of the late Minister's holdings. The old gardener retired and Anders took his place caring for the grounds. Even with his expanded responsibilities, Anders still made time in the afternoons to go with Elsa to the town square to meet the children. He would readily make time to spend with Suzette as well, but her growing list of duties kept her mostly out of sight, except when they convened at the supper table.

One warm spring evening, Suzette found Anders and Elsa outside Anders's cottage. "Have you come to play with us?" Anders asked. "It's been a long time since we've had a game of hide and seek."

"I think I'd rather just talk," Suzette replied.

Anders nodded. Suzette looked too tired for games. Yet, even in her weariness, Anders could easily appreciate what a beautiful woman she had become.

"There's a beautiful moon out tonight," Suzette went on, "and the moonlight is the perfect excuse to get out for a while. I haven't had an evening walk in the gardens since last autumn."

"I know." Anders was very much aware of how long it had been. "We've missed you." He found himself shifting his weight back and forth from foot to foot, as if he'd said something awkward.

"Then it's time to catch up. Take my hand and let's walk like we used to."

Suzette extended her hand to him as she'd done a thousand times before. In those instances, he had taken it readily in simple friendship. Tonight, he hesitated.

As Suzette moved to offer her hand to Anders, her face came into the glow of the moonlight. The weariness vanished. In the moonlight, her face was radiant. Her eyes sparkled with a thousand tiny points of light. She was no longer a child, and taking her hand was no longer a natural action. Now, it was something to be considered. Anders's face became warm as he stood still considering it.

"Come now. Quit wasting time and give me your hand." Suzette took his hand. He felt embarrassed at its clamminess, but she didn't seem to notice.

She dragged him along until he caught up with her. Elsa followed at their heels. "It's so nice to get to spend a little time with my friends. Growing up is so much work. All I hear is 'do this,' 'learn that,' 'mold yourself into a proper lady.' I think I'd rather remain a child forever."

"I'm sorry you have so much work to do," Anders muttered. It was difficult to find the right thing to say because his mind was still contemplating the new way it felt to be holding her hand.

"And that's just the start of it," Suzette continued. "Lately, Mama keeps telling me it's time to start thinking of my future. That means I should worry about finding a husband. I suppose she thinks I'll be an old maid in a few years. I expect to find suitors climbing out of the woodwork any day now."

This talk woke Anders from his reverie. Of course Suzette would be married one day. This was only the natural course of things. Such a beautiful young woman, at her high level of society, would certainly bring many suitors. Anders had never thought of this before. Now that he did think about it, a shiver ran up his spine and he let out an involuntary sigh.

"Is something wrong?" Suzette asked.

"Oh, no," Anders sputtered. "I just caught a chill."

"It's rather a warm night for chills, don't you think?"

"Yes. Rather warm."

"What about you, Anders? You're old enough to be married. Do you ever think about seeking a wife?"

"No. Not really." His voice cracked a little at the end.

"Why not? I thought every man wanted a wife to share his life.

Wouldn't you like that too?"

Anders looked at her and the words flowed out. "I suppose it might be nice."

"Then why don't you go and get one?"

Anders's shoulders slumped. "It's not as easy as that."

"Why not?"

"Well, I don't see many people, outside of the estate."

"But you could, if you wanted to. No one would stop you."

"I'm not much at ease around people."

"I don't believe that. You're at your best among the children."

Anders shrugged. "Around the children, perhaps. Adults are a different story."

"Why should that matter?"

Anders stopped and faced her. "The children don't measure me. They don't stop to calculate what part of a full man I am."

"Oh Anders! You mustn't think that!"

"It's true. The parents don't worry about my influence over their children because they think me just a large child myself."

"If they think that, then they're wrong. You're a better man than any I know."

All at once Anders stood up straight again. His eyes widened in the moonlight. "Do you truly believe that, Suzette?"

"Of course I do. And some woman will be very proud to call you her husband. I have no doubt of it. The only thing lacking is that you haven't met her yet."

Anders's form slackened. "I see," he whispered.

Suzette noticed his deflated tone. "You don't believe it?"

Though he still spoke to her, Anders turned away. "A long time ago, you said I was like a housefly in autumn. You said that because you thought my blood was not thawed out. Well, my blood is thawed by now, but I am more like that housefly in autumn than ever."

"What do you mean?"

"I've outlived my season. I've grown too old for a children's

106

world, but that is the only world that will have me as I am."

She stopped him and took hold of both his hands. "Oh, Anders. Give the adult world a fair chance before you turn your back on it."

Looking into her moonlit eyes, hands in hers, he was helpless to do anything but accept her plea. He agreed to give the adult world its chance, dimly noting that he was held in the hands of that chance even then. Having given her this assurance, they parted, she being quite near the main house and he walking slowly back to his cottage.

All the way back to his cottage, and for some time after reaching it, Anders could not bring a thought to his mind that was not laden with the essence of Suzette. Each thought held a new excitement in it, and a new foreboding. He was sure their friendship would never be the same as it had been, but he was equally confused over whether this change would be for better or worse.

Anders was not familiar with the ways of women, and he did not know how to read between the words Suzette had said. All he knew for certain was that she was no longer the little girl with whom he used to play games. She was grown up now, bright and beautiful, and he was in love with her.

This last revelation scared him. There was a thrill that came with falling in love, but there was also a pain in it. How wonderful it would be to hold her in his arms and feel her soft cheek brush against his. But what chance was there of such things? She was of the highest society and he was an inward-looking gardener without experience at romance. Had she not said the woman meant for him was one he had not yet met?

Then there was the other thing. He had become skilled at keeping it in the background, but it was always there, waiting patiently to come forward. It had always been his refuge to believe Suzette was the one who saw him as a person without pieces missing. That was easy for a little girl to do. But how would a woman rank him among her peers?

The longer he considered his blossoming love, the more the pain overcame the thrill of it. It raised too many questions, with answers too frightening to be pursued. So that he would never need learn the answers, he promised himself he would very carefully hide his love for her away, where it would never be found out.

But, for better or worse, love will not lie buried like so many old dog toys. It was a few weeks later when Anders learned this lesson. It had been such a wonderful surprise when Suzette found him and Elsa in the gardens and invited them to play a game of hide and seek.

"Being grown up all the time is dreadfully wearisome," Suzette explained. "I should like to take a short holiday from it and be a child for just a little while this afternoon." Anders had much work to do, but he could not decline an invitation from Suzette.

It was their best game ever. They lost count of time chasing each other around the grounds, Elsa bouncing happily after, usually giving away Anders's hiding spots. When it was Suzette's last turn to hide, and Anders's last chance to seek, Suzette chose a place among a maze of tall hedges. Anders approached her as she looked in the opposite direction. He crept toward her with such skill that she had no notion he was at hand until he shouted, "I've got you!"

Suzette jumped with fright and surprise. Then, realizing his joke, she turned on him with pretend anger. "How dare you sneak up on me like that? You scared me half to death!" she exclaimed between giggles, playfully beating her fists against his chest.

It might have been the gentle tapping over his heart or the light shining from her smiling eyes that awakened the emotion in him. For the first time since he was pulled from the icy lake all those years ago, his reflexes were swift. Before he, she, or any power on earth, could prevent it, he had taken her shoulders into his hands and placed a quick peck of a kiss on her lips.

For a moment the world swayed in the balance. The expression on her face said nothing—neither good nor bad. In that moment, it seemed like all the people in the world put down their labors and took note that a man had unexpectedly kissed a woman.

In the next moment, the world started up again. People returned

108

to their toils and the betting wheel of emotions inside Suzette settled on panic. Anders's insides turned to stone as he watched a quiver in her lips turn into an uncontrollable shake throughout her entire body. Escape, her eyes said, so it is no wonder she turned and fled as swiftly as she was able.

"No! Wait! Don't go!" he yelled, running after her. "I'm sorry. Please, forgive me! Please!" Although he had the legs to overtake her, he lacked the heart. When he saw that words would not stop her, he gave up the chase and fell to his knees in the grass.

"What have I done?" he shouted to no one. "What have I done? Let her forgive me. Oh, God, let her forgive me!" He pitched himself prone on the ground.

Elsa, sensitive to his sadness, lay down beside him. Feeling her near, he lifted his eyes to those of what could well be the only friend that remained to him. "How could I do such a thing?" he asked, as if one who by nature loved unconditionally could understand the strange fragility of human relationships. To Elsa, it was a senseless question. Her philosophy was too sensible for human understanding. In reply she licked his face compassionately. "You are," he said with a frown, "the only girl in this world who would willingly kiss me." She licked his face again.

CHAPTER 27

Anders rested his cheek on the handle of his spade. For three days he had been doing more leaning on his digging tools than gardening. It was impossible to remember that disastrous kiss and concentrate on work at the same time. Since he could not stop recalling that kiss, his work suffered.

He straightened up for a moment, dug a few weeds from between the favored plants, then settled his cheek back on the wooden handle. Neither he nor his work could continue in this way, but he could not free himself of this cycle of regret. The passing days didn't seem to be helping.

At last it was time to visit the school children at the fountain. He put away his tools with relief. In three days, only the time spent telling stories to the children had soothed his mind of the haunting caused by that misguided kiss. For an hour, he might find refuge from the vision of that horrible moment.

The time spent with the children was a relief, but it ended all too soon. Back at his cottage, one of the house servants knocked on his door to deliver his supper. He had not dared go to the main house for a meal since his misdeed. It was hard enough to find his appetite here, with only Elsa's sympathetic eyes to watch him.

It would be impossible to eat a single morsel under the gaze of Suzette's angry eyes. It would be impossible to do anything but throw himself at her feet and beg forgiveness. He contemplated that very act every night as he struggled to swallow a few mouthfuls of food. He would do it in an instant if he could be sure she would forgive him. Lacking that assurance, it was impossible to contemplate being in her presence at all.

Anders put a morsel of bread into his mouth and chewed for a long time without swallowing. Instead of the little table spread before him he saw a vision of the grand table in the main dining room. He envisioned begging Suzette's forgiveness a thousand times over. Each

110

time he begged, Suzette's response was different. It was angry; it was disappointed; it was hurt by the broken bond of friendship. Once, it was genuinely forgiving, but mixed in with the other outcomes, the chance of forgiveness was too small to be trusted.

Yet, he must find a way to apologize to her. As the breaker of their sacred trust, it was only right that he do so. If only he could bear the idea of seeing what was written in her eyes, this might be possible. Until then, the shame he felt must surely render him speechless in her presence.

Taking a drink to wash down the troublesome bread, he decided he would attempt a note of apology to her. Certainly, her eyes could not make the paper forget its words. It was safer than facing her. He pushed his food out of the way and took up pen and paper.

It was short and simple, but it took hours, and many drafts, to compose. He struggled to get the tone just right, and in the end he was still not satisfied. But he had done his best.

> Dear friend Suzette, If I could have but one wish to come true in my life, it would be that you could forgive me. That is all I want. Please, please, forgive me. Your friendship is everything to me. If I lost it, my heart and soul would surely die. I only ask another chance to prove myself worthy of it. Please. Your friend forever, no matter should you hate me,
> Anders.
> P.S. I know I was a fool to think you could ever love one such as me.

He folded the note and secretly placed it where she, and only she, would be sure to find it.

The next morning found him more useless at his work than ever. It was a relief to have taken action, but the action he'd taken terrified him. To work, or to do anything other than imagine the moment when the words on the paper revealed themselves to Suzette's mind, was not possible.

At last, Anders gave up the fiction of gardening. He cast his latest unused tool aside and sat on the ground, resting his head in his hands. Elsa was immediately at hand, lying with her chin at his knee.

Anders stroked Elsa's head. "Do you think she found it yet?" he asked.

Elsa looked up at him with soft eyes that counseled patience.

"What if she never finds it? Maybe something moved it out of sight. I should have done a better job of making sure she'd find it."

Elsa rolled her head a bit to the side.

"You're right," Anders told her. "She's sure to find it. But maybe she'll rip it up. If she's as angry as she has the right to be, she may not read it at all."

Elsa blinked.

Anders gasped. "What if she's reading it at this very moment? Is she cursing the day she met such a false friend?" He swallowed hard. "Or is she laughing? Is she laughing at the simpleton who dared kiss her and then dared ask forgiveness?"

Elsa shook her head out from under Anders's trembling hand.

"Yes. You're right," Anders said to her. "That's not like her. No matter how much she hates me, she wouldn't laugh."

That evening Anders discovered a letter, slipped under his door while he was out. The handwriting was unmistakably hers. He picked up the paper, feeling lightheaded as he unfolded the page. His hands shook as he read.

> *Anders, my dearest and lifelong friend,*
> *I can't imagine how I could ever grow to*
> *hate you, for I have loved you as dearly as I*
> *could have loved a doting, older brother, had*
> *I one. You have always been my hero, and*

ever shall you be a hero to me. You need never fear losing my friendship should you still wish it. You may not find me worthy of your friendship by the time you finish this letter.

My dear Anders, if you feel you must seek forgiveness from me, of course, you have it. The evil you imagine yourself to have done is as nothing when measured against what I have done. You think that I have not come to you of late because I could not face you. In this you are correct. You think that I could not face you because I was angry. Again you are correct. But where your line of reasoning fails is in believing that my anger is for you. My anger is all for myself. I have done years of wrong to you. Only when you did that which now brings you so much remorse, did I realize the disservice I have long done you. The question now is whether you can forgive me.

Since the very beginnings of our friendship, I have always considered myself your most eager and sincere defender against those who so much as intimated you were anything less than other men. I would not allow anyone, no matter who they might be, to make an issue of your slow speech or deliberate thought. Why was I so eager to argue that you were no different from any other man? Of course, you were my best

113

friend, and I owed you my life. But above all that, I believed it. I was sure I believed it.

Upon reflection, it seems quite natural that you should develop romantic feelings for me. I am the only woman in whose presence you were allowed to feel at ease. It follows that your human desire to be loved would bring you to me. I hold nothing against your feelings. It is my feelings that trouble me. You see, now I begin to wonder why I did not fall in love with you. You are the sweetest, kindest person I have ever known, and I love you dearly. You have ever been the very essence of courage, bravery, and tenderness—all that is exemplary about manhood. Yet thoughts of you and thoughts of romance have never mingled within my mind. In these past days, I have asked myself again and again why I have not fallen in love with you. Each time, I avoid the answer, for I fear I cannot live well with it.

So, you see, it is you that I ask to forgive me. I have treated you falsely through all the years. I can only imagine the tremendous hurt I am causing you even at this moment. But I feel I must let you know the truth so that you might see who is the real villain. Dear, sweet Anders, I hope you will always allow me your friendship, for I love you with all my heart. That I cannot be in love with you is my failing, not yours. Your friend *forever, I pray.*

Suzette.

*P.S. Please take your supper at the house
tomorrow. It would mean the world to me.*

When Anders finished the letter, he set it gently down on the desk and continued to stare at it. Eventually, his head fell into his hands and he wept, happy that his treasured friendship was saved, but also with a dark heart, knowing the one he loved could never love him back in the same manner.

Elsa rested her chin across his knee. She was the only one left in the world who saw him as a man unequaled by all others.

CHAPTER 28

When Anders entered the room, Suzette was already seated at the table. Usually, Suzette and her mother came to dine together, but this evening the mother's chair was empty.

Anders took his normal seat, across the table from Suzette. Each avoided looking at the other's face. "Where is your mother?" Anders asked in a voice that only barely made itself heard.

"She's not feeling well, so she had her supper taken to her room," Suzette answered without lifting her eyes from the tablecloth.

"It's nothing serious, I hope," remarked Anders.

"No. Just a little headache."

Anders gave the plate in front of him all his attention. "That's good. I mean, that it's nothing serious."

"Yes, I'm glad it's not serious," Suzette agreed.

"Me too," Anders repeated.

It was a strain paying so much attention to things on the table. All at once, the force holding their eyes down snapped. Their heads bobbed up in unison and their eyes met. As they looked into each other's faces, both blurted out the words, "I'm sorry."

They fidgeted, each searching for the words to say next. A butler brought in a tray and set soup down before each of them. Even had they found words, they would scarcely have spoken them in front of a third person. The silence continued until the intruder left. By then they had been quiet so long they both felt the ridiculousness of it.

In the face of this awkwardness, Anders took refuge in the only place he could find—behind a smile. Relieved, Suzette smiled back. She took the next step by beginning to chuckle. Anders chuckled back at her. The next instant found them laughing into each other's faces. It was an uplifting, cleansing laugh.

"Friends should always be able to laugh together," Suzette said.

"Always," Anders agreed.

"Let's always be best friends," Suzette suggested.

"Always."

The laughter was gone, but it had done its work. Suzette looked him in the eye. "No matter what is meant for us, in our separate lives, I will always know that your friendship will come shining through like gold."

"So too will yours, no matter what happens in our separate lives." Anders stressed the part about separate lives to prove he had overcome any feelings beyond simple friendship he previously entertained.

But he had not overcome them. He was in love with her. That was not the sort of thing that could be swept away with a hearty laugh. Though being in love with her was not a profitable course to take, nothing in him had the power to alter that course. A man's mind may not use reason to persuade his heart, for his heart will take no stock in mere logic.

What he did have the power to do was hide his feelings from her. This is what he was determined to do. He would show her the friendly face of the brother she thought him. Before he first dipped his spoon into his soup, he vowed to never speak to her in the vague, circular puzzles frustrated young men use to hint their feelings in the constant twilight of undying hope. He would never put her through the agony of enduring a forlorn stammer from him.

Anders and Suzette finished the meal in the comfort of renewed friendship. Even so, as time passed, they found themselves less often together. Suzette took over more of the duties of managing the estate from her mother. Besides that, it was time for her to surrender to the demands of polite society. Polite society laid many demands on such a well-bred young lady.

Hard work during the daytime and a busy social calendar at night left Suzette little time for her old playmates. Lacking her company, Anders grew melancholy. In the daytime he had his work to occupy him. But in the evenings, especially after Suzette became frequently absent from the supper table, loneliness overtook him.

As if his present sadness weren't enough, he realized that one day

Suzette would marry, giving her dearest affections to another, leaving him with whatever occasional greetings and faded memories were left. He would slip from being her best friend to being an old friend.

These thoughts brought him pain, and the pain brought stories to his mind—stories of flowers and animals and love and sadness, and even happiness, for great sadness makes one know that there is such a thing somewhere called happiness, even though it may be hiding far away.

To keep his mind occupied through the evenings, Anders wrote down the stories he'd told the children. They were simple stories, and that was the value in them. They made simple points and illustrated simple lessons, their wisdom untarnished by complexity.

It was not uncommon for Anders to talk to himself as he wrote down the stories. It helped him find the most fitting words if he spoke the story aloud, just as he had done with the children. But some nights, his solitary dialogue drifted away from the events of the story. This occurred when telling the story brought Anders closer to the dark door in his mind behind which lay the light of his former genius.

As he sat, twirling his quill between his fingers and letting the story he wrote slip to the back of his mind, Anders spoke to himself. "I'm closer to that door now, closer to passing through it into the light that once was mine. I'll have that light again, some day. I must; it so much feels as though I must."

He lay his pen down and stared into a distant corner of the room. "I'm making something from nothing. That's the same as I used to do. When I write these things down, I know they are something. Are they useful things? I don't know. But it is something from nothing; there must be value in that. At least, it is one step back in the direction of the life I was meant for."

The hint of a smile touched his face. "When I write I see flashes. I feel nearly like the person I once was. For an instant, I am he who had not yet left his potential drowned beneath the ice."

Anders reached out his hands. Then his little smile turned to a frown and he let his arms drop. "There are moments when I think I can reach out and touch that man, but the image always fades before I can put my hands to it."

He slouched into his chair and shook his head at himself. "The nearness of him is maddening." He sat up straight and took hold of his pen. "I can't give up. There's still time. Perhaps it's a fanciful dream, but it feels as real as this quill in my hand. If I can recapture that man, then maybe . . ." He made no mention of fortune or fame. "If I can do it, then my position is completely changed with her. She'll have to look at me in a different light."

The next day, Anders made a trip to the university to seek out his old professors. The oldest of the three had died, but the other two were still there. Anders went first to the one who had been most impatient for him to complete his great manuscript in those years past.

The professor fell over himself when he recognized Anders; he had settled it in his mind that he would never see this former student at the university again. When Anders spoke to him, he was taken aback all the more.

"I have come to collect my manuscript," Anders told him.

"You will return to university to work?" asked the professor with wide eyes.

"No," Anders replied. "I have no place here. I will work on my own."

The professor's eyes narrowed. He had suffered a bitter loss of recognition when his student failed to become famous. Now, this same student would reach for that glorious end without him. "It's been so long. I don't know where the manuscript is to be found. Most likely it is misplaced and not to be found by the most thorough of searches."

Anders was well enough versed in storytelling to sense that these statements fell short of the truth. "It may be so," he replied, "but I will ask the university archivist to make a search just the same."

The professor frowned. "Even if, by chance, the manuscript were located, you could not take it. Recall that you abandoned it years ago.

119

After all this time, it is the property of the university. The university is not in the habit of lending its property to just anyone."

Though the professor's last sentence stung him, Anders made no reply. He let his head fall and walked away with the slow gait of a disappointed man.

As soon as this professor was out of sight, Anders hurried to seek out the other of his erstwhile mentors. There was no guarantee that the other professor would not also block his plan, but it hurt nothing for Anders to try him. To the second professor he told his plan, and of the resistance with which it had been met.

The professor sat for a long time, considering the situation. He seemed less hurt that he had missed his chance at the coattails of fame. At last he nodded to himself. "Come," he said to Anders, and leading the way into the archive, retrieved the dust-covered volume. Handing the text to Anders, he said, "I only pray I am doing right, for in truth, I fear the result of my actions."

"I am sorry to bring the displeasure of your colleague upon you," replied Anders.

"You misunderstand. I don't fear what he may think. We have no right to hold this from you. Beneath his hurt feelings, he knows that. The result I fear is the one I may be bringing to you. Collecting dust in our archive, this manuscript does us no good, but it does you no harm. There is something mournful in unfinished work. I pray you do not let this fragment of a manuscript make you mourn the rest of your life."

Anders had no reply for this. In his heart, he knew he was betting against all odds in revisiting his old manuscript. But he had already concluded that even simple gardeners must wager liberally when the prize is so great.

CHAPTER 29

Anders took a deep breath and steeled himself. He gazed around the room, seeking comfort in the familiar surroundings of his cottage. Leaning forward, he took another breath and turned back the pages of the manuscript to the beginning.

He had toiled over it every evening, forbidding himself to become discouraged by the burden of sustaining a narrative more intricate than a fairy tale. Never did he let anyone, especially Suzette, know he had resumed work on his manuscript. Only after he had proved he could complete the work with as much skill as he'd begun it would he share his accomplishment with her. Then, she'd have to see him as a whole man. Then, she could love him as he loved her.

When Anders finally laid down his pen to judge his progress, two years had passed. In those two years, he never once dared compare the old portion of the manuscript with the additions he made. Despite his fears, he worked on the faith that some miraculous power within the universe, or perhaps even within himself, would match the quality of his new writing with the old.

Anders's faithfulness to his work was matched by his discipline regarding his feelings for Suzette. That his love for her lived unabated was a secret known only to himself. Neither by word nor deed did he give Suzette the smallest clue that his thoughts of her went beyond the realm of simple friendship.

Suzette had put Anders's one disastrous foray beyond the bounds of friendship out of her mind. She was content to believe any romantic impulses Anders once had were a passing infatuation. This infatuation, she convinced herself, had long ago run its course, withered, and died, leaving their friendship stronger than ever.

It had not withered in the least. Anders spent all his time quietly working toward the day when he might open his heart once more. The next time he offered his love to Suzette, he would not be a common gardener. He'd be an accomplished man of letters. When he showed his feelings again, the glory surrounding them would be irresistible.

Anders finally reached a turning point in his work. In order to go on, he must go back and review the entire manuscript from the start. His hands shook as he began. His stomach tied itself in knots as he read. The knots grew ever tighter until they snapped and his stomach fell. This cataclysm came at the transition from old to the new portions of the work.

It was as if the story and all the characters had fallen off a high cliff.

Anders squeezed his forehead in his hand. "Ugh!" he cried. "The new part is nothing more than a series of tales, unrelated to the older part. The only connection is that the characters bear the same names." There was none of the complexity or layering of the earlier portion. "This is not a master work," he moaned. "It's not even a minor work!" It was merely a study in contrasts.

It was now clear to him that no matter what he attempted, what he achieved were simple, short tales that would prove nothing to Suzette or anyone else. He stared at the ink on the paper. The words formed by that ink were inadequate, and always would be.

"Two years!" he growled at himself. "Two years working as hard as I know how. For nothing! Wasted!" But that was not the worst part. "Two years? I would spend 20 years. I have nothing but time. Gladly, I would spend 20 years if there were any hope of getting it right. But there is none. The work is pointless. The future is hopeless. I've lost her. The devil can have those two years, and the next 20 to boot."

As Anders sat considering his future, the door to his cottage swung inward and Suzette burst into the house, as she was wont to do whenever she had exciting news to share with her friend. Now that she was a grown woman, she was driven to Anders by her excitement less frequently than when she was a child, but the child in her was not yet wholly tamed.

"Anders! Oh, Anders!" she cried with delight. "I'm so happy to find you here! You must guess my news before another moment has gone by! Go on," she squealed with childish delight. "Guess what has happened!"

Anders was not in the mood for guessing games, and besides, he had no idea what Suzette's news might be. He shook his head. "I can't guess," he said.

Suzette began to pout. "Oh, do try. Just one guess."

Anders rubbed his temple. "I have no idea."

Suzette sighed. "Very well. Perhaps it's unfair to make you guess. I'll tell you. Are you ready?"

Anders nodded.

"I'm to be married! Isn't it wonderful? I came to tell you just as quick as I could. I've fallen in love and I'm going to be married!"

Anders sat still as a stone. His heart fell down with his stomach. A thousand feelings fought his stillness, wanting to scream their way out of him. He held himself tightly, and kept them all inside.

Two years ago, it would have been cruel of Suzette to throw the news at him in this giddy fashion. Anders did such an exceptional job of hiding his feelings during those years that Suzette felt no hesitation at filling Anders's house with her exuberance. In her mind, there was nothing between them that should give her pause.

For the sake of her happiness, Anders took the ruse to a higher level of deception. After a moment spent collecting himself, he smiled and hugged her as if this were the happiest news she could have brought him. Only the keenest observer would have doubted that he shared her joy completely. All the while he held the myriad pieces of his heart together only by the extraordinary power of his will.

After she acquainted him with every bit of minutiae surrounding her impending nuptials, she grew more calm. "There is," she told him, "one arrangement yet to be made. It requires that I ask a great favor of you."

"Whatever you ask of me, you shall have."

"Be careful of what you grant unknowing. I ask a great deal." She took his hand in hers. "But let me tell you what it is. I want you to take the place that would have been for Papa. I want you to bless the union by giving away my hand in marriage." Anders could not respond at once; all his effort was needed to prevent his heart from bursting.

"I realize," she continued, "I am asking the world of you, but I have been thinking lately about the very first story you ever told me. Do you remember? It was the story of the sweetest rose, and how it was granted the place of highest honor at the princess's wedding. I am no princess, but you are the sweetest rose. You have always been the sweetest, best friend I could ever have hoped for, and I want you to have the place of highest honor at my wedding."

As much as Anders's soul resisted the idea of giving Suzette to another man, he could not refuse her. To do so risked the humiliation of revealing his true feelings again. Beyond this, a simmering guilt asked Anders if it were not he who was responsible for the fact that Suzette had no father to give her hand at marriage. Though he had been absolved of responsibility long ago, by the one most able to absolve him, he had never fully absolved himself. If this were the price for his cowardly silence those years ago, he must pay it. "As I said, whatever you ask of me, you shall have."

She threw her arms around him. "My happiness is complete." As she hugged him, she chanced to look over his shoulder at the work spread out on his table. She let him go and pointed at the papers. "My, you certainly have kept busy. You never kept such papers when I used to be always in and out of your house. What's all this?"

Anders stepped between her and the table. "Nothing. Nothing at all. Merely a passing fancy. I was just tidying up."

"Oh," she said. "I half hoped it meant you had secretly returned to your studies."

Anders cast his eyes away from her. "That's all behind me now," he assured her.

"Maybe someday you'll try it again."

"Maybe."

For the first time in his life Anders was relieved when Suzette left him. His mask was rapidly slipping. No sooner had she gone than it fell away. He fell limp into a chair. At once, the chin of the always responsive Elsa was at his knee, her compassionate eyes seeking his. He put a hand on her head. "Did the sweetest rose feel any pain when cut for its place of honor at the princess's wedding?" he asked her.

As these words escaped him, Anders's attention returned to the manuscript on the table. He walked to the table and stared down at the place he had stopped before Suzette came. Everything in the world had changed since he had looked up from that page. Everything had changed except the manuscript itself. "It was worthless then, and it is worthless now," he muttered. Then he closed his manuscript with the gentle hand of sadness and placed it carefully atop the shelf to sit untouched by his overreaching dreams.

CHAPTER 30

Anders smiled into the looking glass, silently counting 10 before letting his face relax. That one was good. No one would see through it. After an hour of practicing, the mirror assured him he'd gotten it right. There would be nothing but happiness written across his face on the day of the wedding.

He'd try one more smile, just to make sure it was right. He peered into the glass again and had counted to five when he was interrupted by a gentle rapping at his door. Like a child playing at something naughty, Anders scurried to hide the looking glass before going to open the door.

Waiting on the opposite side of his threshold were Suzette and a young man of Anders's own age, or perhaps a few years older. The two stood with arms locked. Suzette beamed with pride. The man was handsome and wore the outfit of a well-to-do gentleman. Altogether, his appearance was smart and his demeanor one of self-confidence.

Suzette spoke in a delighted tone. "Mr. Anders Christiansen, I give you my fiancée, Mr. Friedrich Helgaard." The two men bowed and exchanged greetings. "I'm sorry to have come unannounced," Suzette explained, "but I couldn't wait to introduce you."

Anders nodded his understanding.

"I thought you would like to meet the man you are giving my hand to," Suzette went on. "If it's not an inconvenience, I thought I'd leave you to become acquainted."

Anders used the smile he had recently mastered. "Of course. It's no inconvenience at all. Won't you come in, Mr. Helgaard?"

"Thank you," Mr. Helgaard replied. He stopped for a quick kiss on the cheek from Suzette, then removed his top hat and followed his host inside.

"Please make yourself comfortable. May I bring you some refreshment, Mr. Helgaard?" Anders asked when they were alone.

"Please don't trouble yourself. I'm quite content merely to sit and

126

talk. And please call me Fred. You are such a dear friend of Suzette's; I feel as if you are my friend already." When they were both seated, Fred began the conversation. "I trust you have been provided with everything you need for the ceremony."

"Oh yes, indeed," Anders replied. "Just the other day I received a new suit of clothes. I've never seen one finer. I hardly feel equal to wearing it."

"I have no doubt you will do it justice."

"And a whole troop of ladies and gentlemen have led me about, telling me where to stand and what to do."

Fred smiled. "The same group have led me about. If you begin to feel like a herded sheep, believe me, you're not alone. But, I suppose there's no escaping it. Their intentions are good."

Anders nodded. "They've been very patient with me."

"And I'm sure you've made it easy on them."

"I've tried my best, but I do get a little nervous. I've never stood before a large crowd before, except for children."

"I know you'll do fine."

Anders sighed. "I hope so. I'd hate to make a mistake at Suzette's wedding, though people might expect it of me."

Fred shook his head and smiled. "If anyone makes a mistake I bet it's me."

Anders seemed not to hear this attempt at reassurance. "If it were anyone but Suzette, I'd be tempted to send my regrets. But for her, I will gladly risk what little esteem I have with the rest of the world."

"She is that important to you?"

"Yes."

"You mean the same to her. She speaks of you often—of what you did for her and of all the wonderful memories she has of playing in the gardens with you." Fred's air of self-confidence faded. "This is why I wanted to ask you the question that has been nagging me."

"What question?"

Fred rubbed his face. "Well, I don't know exactly how to put it.

127

You see, I have been quite successful in business. I can give Suzette anything she wants, in material things. But my business is centered a great distance from here, and it requires that I go abroad frequently. I could not bear to leave Suzette behind when I travel."

Anders nodded along without any clue where Fred's words were leading.

"I love Suzette madly. I want to marry her more than anything. But this place is all she's ever known. She adores this place, and the people here. I'm not sure I can make her give up everything she's ever loved in trade for her love for me."

"Maybe she would like to travel. Have you asked her?"

"Yes. Many times. She always says she wants only to be my wife and she would go wherever I take her, but the way she talks about this place, and about you, I wonder if her heart would always be here."

The reference to himself brought down all of Anders's practiced facial expressions. He found himself biting his lip.

"I couldn't take her into my world, knowing she truly wished to remain here," Fred continued. "You know her better than anyone. I place my trust completely in your hands. Am I doing her injustice by marrying her and taking her away from here? Is it better for her that I go away and leave her to the world she loves best?"

It was an enormous question. Anders's lips trembled and his eyes watered. "You love her with all your heart?"

"My entire heart," came the quick reply.

"And she loves you in the same way?"

"I'm certain she does."

This was the opportunity a rival prays for; Anders's hands and feet shook at the chance it offered. But Anders was not Fred's rival. He was Suzette's friend. "Then place your trust completely in your own hands, and in hers. She is not a child. You can believe her when she tells you what she wants. Marry her." His head drooped with these last two words as though they had taken every bit of his strength.

Fred did not fail to notice how Anders's mouth trembled or how red and moist his eyes had become. "You really love her, don't you?" he asked.

Anders held his breath. After all this time of hiding his love away, had this new acquaintance seen right through him in the space of only minutes? Of all people, must it be her fiancée?

Fred did not wait for Anders to catch his breath. "It's clear you do. I don't wonder why she chose you to give her hand in marriage. You love her as if she were your own child."

Anders breathed. "She is very dear to me," he said with a little gasp of relief.

"She is fortunate to have had you."

The past-tense statement stung Anders. She would need him no more, now that she would have a husband. "I was the fortunate one," he said.

After Fred said goodbye, Anders retrieved his looking glass. His countenance was in a disappointing state. He must do better than this at the ceremony. If he couldn't keep up the façade of a smile, at least he must practice weeping in a fatherly way.

He practiced every day until the wedding. As he did so, he also practiced at preparing himself for the reality of Suzette going away as another man's bride. It was more difficult to judge his progress at this. Only the wedding day would reveal the magnitude of his success or failure.

Soon enough, that day was at hand. Hundreds of guests waited in anticipation. Anders donned his fine new suit, looking so dapper that anyone might have guessed it was his own wedding day. But Anders was taking the bride to the altar today, not away from it.

Just before Anders was to walk Suzette down the aisle, he pulled from his pocket a rose of deep red. "I searched all the gardens," he told her. "This is the sweetest smelling rose of them all."

Suzette took the rose and put it to her nose. She breathed in its fragrance. "No rose could smell sweeter," she said. "It smells of sweet friendship, a dear friendship that will live forever and always. Help me put it into my hair."

Suzette's hair had been planned out for weeks in advance by the leading experts in the field. Every strand and every accessory had been perfectly placed. Inserting such an unanticipated item as a fresh rose haphazardly within this carefully considered sculpture was very near to a scandalous act. Nonetheless, Suzette welcomed the intrusion as Anders carefully slid the short stem of the rose into her hair above her ear.

"How does it look?" she asked when he had taken his hand away.

"It looks beautiful," he said.

"I'll keep it always," she told him. "The sweetest rose from my sweetest friend."

"When you look at it, remember how much I . . ." He cleared his throat softly and shook his head the tiniest little bit. "Remember how much I was always your friend."

"I won't need anything to remind me of that," she assured him. Then the bridal procession began.

They started down the aisle. It was a long walk for a man who must keep his head held high with so many forces at work making him want to bow it down. And then, all too soon, it was over. They were at the altar. For a fleeting instant, Anders alone held the hand he loved. Then, as was his duty, he placed that hand into the hand of another, and put himself off to the side.

The ceremony was magnificent. The guests were accommodated in high style, and there was even a special place for Elsa. Throughout the remainder of the day Anders stood exactly where he was supposed to stand, did just as he was supposed to do, and said everything he was supposed to say. He smiled genuinely and made gracious comments, letting no one guess that he had just placed the love of his life into the hands of another.

After the ceremony, many guests made a point to congratulate him on the flawless performance of his duties. When it was over, Suzette gave him a long, warm hug. "You were wonderful today!" she said into his ear.

"You have always been wonderful," he said back to her. Then, fearing how she might interpret this, he added, "My dear friend."

Shortly thereafter, the bride and groom were whisked off in a stately carriage to begin their new lives together. The guests went home, and the day faded into evening.

At night, when Anders was home again, and there were no more human eyes to watch, his practiced emotions fell away. He slipped into the pit of melancholy. Now the day began to take its revenge on him. Suzette was gone to live in a far-off city where her husband had his business. Meanwhile, Anders was left to exist here forevermore, without a heart, for she had taken his with her. He was, he believed, hereafter cut off from any hope of true human love, which is to say he was cut off from hope.

Elsa sensed his melancholy and tried to comfort him, but he would not be comforted. He would not stand still, nor make himself easy to approach. He wrung his hands and clutched his head, walking to and fro, with no purpose whatever. His eyes sped around the room as if searching for some sacred object, but they found nothing, for they knew not the thing for which they searched. There must be something. There must be something that would make the sun rise again.

In the midst of his despair, as he was pacing about the main room, Anders's eye found the unconquerable manuscript he had shelved. For a moment, the manuscript seemed to have a voice of its own. "I could have won her," it told him. "But you? You are not worthy of me, and therefore, not worthy of her. Remember when you were a man? You could have won her then, with ease. And now? Now you are a child. A woman needs a man, not a boy. Of course you could not have her. You will have no one!"

In a fit of fury, like nothing that had ever possessed him, Anders ripped the manuscript from the shelf and flung it into the fire burning in the hearth. This brought no relief; the object was merely a symbol. The words it spoke came from his own mind. Now they came from his own mouth. "Who could love me?" he screamed, spitting the question in the direction of Elsa's frightened eyes. "Who could even count me as a whole person? Who?"

Elsa, unaccustomed to such rage, watched with worried eyes, but she did not approach as usual.

"Damn you!" he scolded. "Why didn't you just let me drown?"

With this the storm passed. His fury had burnt itself out. He fell into his chair as the rage drained from him. Elsa, reading the change, at last approached. When he felt her near, he gently took her face in his hands and put his forehead to hers. "Forgive me," he cried. "I know who. I know so well. You give a hundredfold more than you ask. But man is a greedy animal, and sometimes it is just not enough."

CHAPTER 31

As Anders worked at writing down his day's fairy tale, Elsa came to him as she often did. She rested her chin on his thigh and looked up at his face with her soft, brown eyes. Anders put a hand on her head and petted her gently.

"You know, I was thinking," he said as he petted her ears. "These two years since Suzette was married have not been so bad as I feared they would be. In a way, I'm glad it's all done and over with."

She gazed up at him with her soft eyes to show she was listening.

"It's a relief to be writing down these simple children's stories. I don't get nervous over them like I did over the work I used to attempt. And if Suzette were still here and unmarried, I'd likely be tearing my hair out, trying to prove I can still do what I'm not able to any longer. In a sense, she put an end to my misery by getting married and going away."

Elsa seemed to nod with her eyes.

"I do miss her though," Anders went on. "Even when she comes to visit and we talk about old times, it's not the same. Her heart is far away, in her new life, even when she is here. That's the natural way of things, I suppose, but it still makes me sad."

He looked down into her eyes and smiled. "Which is why I rely upon you more than ever. You carry me through solitude." It was true. He did look to her to soothe the loneliness of his life. Elsa was eager to take on as much of the burden of Anders's heart as he was willing to give her. She didn't care if he spoke slowly. If he should forget all the words he ever knew, he would still be the best man who ever lived as far as she was concerned. He was her world.

Usually, she might let him pet her for a long time. Tonight she slid her head out from under his hand.

She did not normally lick him unless she sensed he was in a mood of particular melancholy. Tonight, she licked his hand, though he felt perfectly content. Anders, knowing her habits so well, shook his head.

"I'm really quite all right," he assured her.

She blinked her eyes at him, as if to say, "I know you are." Then she went over to her corner bed and curled up into a ball to sleep.

In relying upon Elsa more than ever, Anders ignored nature. In the time it had taken for Suzette to grow up and marry, Elsa had gone from a young dog to an old one.

Now, all of her days counted against her. Anders, who might well have foreseen how nature would treat a dog differently than a man, would not face the truth. Having lost all others dear to him, he could not bring himself to countenance the ironclad rules of time. The blow that awaited was not softened, as it might have been had he recognized its approach.

An hour later, when Anders went to wish Elsa goodnight before going to bed himself, she was perfectly still. Not so much as a feeble breath escaped her. She had said her goodbyes.

He buried her behind his cottage. For two days he did not eat. For three nights, he slept on the grass beside her grave. Since he had first begun telling stories to Suzette and her schoolmates in the square, he had never missed two consecutive days of meeting the children there. Now, he didn't go for two weeks. When Suzette learned the mournful news, she sent him money with which to buy an engraved stone. This helped lift his spirits, but not enough to keep his eyes dry through an entire evening.

Anders spent the hour he normally gave to the children sitting by Elsa's grave. He brought freshly cut flowers with him every day and busied himself winding their stems to make a new arrangement each time. This he did in silence every day until the last day of the fortnight.

On this day, though there was no one nearby, he spoke. Kneeling on the grass, twining his flowers, he addressed his words to Elsa. "I have been thinking a lot these days," he said. "I have been thinking about life and fate. And I have been thinking about you."

He arranged the flowers against the stone Suzette had purchased. "You found me because I needed you. I was not strong enough to cope with my fate. I needed you to hold me up."

He collected yesterday's flowers, piling them on the grass. "I've been prone to self-pity. Since the accident, I've always been afraid of the future. I've tried to run back to the past. It doesn't work."

"I hated the man I've become. I sought only to return to who I once was, but I always failed. And you were always there to pick me up. But you couldn't go on picking me up forever. I understand that now."

Anders smoothed out the dirt mound of her grave with his hand. "You did your work. You held me up until I could stand on my own. I'm ready to stand now. I am who I am. I accept that. What has been, has been. What will be, will be. I can't go back, so I will go forward. I will stand tall, and I will take my fate as it comes. I will make the best of it. You need not worry. I've learned how to stand on my own two feet."

Anders sat back on his heels and surveyed his work. He nodded approval at the way the flowers looked. "I'm going to go back, tomorrow, and tell stories to the children again," he said to the mound before him. "If they haven't all abandoned me by now, that is. I look forward to their company. It makes me happy."

He shook his head at a memory of himself. "I've been afraid to admit it when I'm happy. I thought I shouldn't be happy until I had again become the person I once was. But I know now that it would mean I would never be happy. I want to be happy. I really do."

Anders slowly rose to his feet. "So," he continued, "I am going to stop trying so hard to go backward in time. It's a tempting thing to want to do, but it robs from the present. Instead, I will take the days as they come, and do my best to find happiness in them as they are. I am still here, after all, and that is something of a miracle. If I am grateful for that miracle, maybe I will be more satisfied with the man I am."

"I am going to look forward now. I think that was something you always tried to teach me to do. I want you to know that I have learned. Whenever I needed saving, you saved me, and I am forever grateful. I take your leaving as a sign that I won't need to be saved again."

Anders stooped to pick up the pile of yesterday's flowers. They were so much less vibrant than today's flowers. As he went to throw them away, he realized how much easier words came to him since he had stopped trying so hard to command them in the way he had before his accident.

As he promised, Anders returned to the town square and won back his entire audience. Still, all was not exactly the same as before. Whether or not the children noticed, the stories he told covered a fuller spectrum of emotion. They were both more lonely and more hopeful. They were not wrecked pieces of a former greatness; they were the building stones of a future greatness.

The children loved the stories more than ever. They did not know it, but there was something extra added to these tales. There was a new satisfaction in these yarns. Before, these children's stories had been a mere link to something greater, breadcrumbs to mark the way to the real reward. Now, they were something worthwhile in themselves. They were the treasure all around. They were the kind of stories that could live forever.

Chapter 32

People who live in solitude often find comfort in routine. Routine keeps their minds occupied. It spares them the boredom that leads to loneliness.

At night, after his work in the gardens was done, Anders wrote the stories he told the children down on paper. He couldn't say exactly why he did this. Never in all his life did he show them to another soul. More than anything else, writing his stories down on paper at night was a comfortable routine.

During the 25 years after Elsa said her last farewell to Anders, he amassed a volume of papers. In all that time, those papers did nothing more than collect dust on his shelf. They contained diversions for the children, and to the handful of children who heard the stories from his lips, they were a delight. That alone made them worthwhile.

The passing years brought significant changes. Suzette had raised three children. Suzette's mother could no longer manage on her own and went to live with Suzette, putting the estate of the late Minister of the Exchequer up for sale.

Anders was offered a place with Suzette's family, but he couldn't imagine living among old dreams and new surroundings. When the Church purchased the Minister's estate for a school, assurances were made that Anders would be allowed to stay in his cottage and work as groundskeeper.

In this, the Church was true to its word. Anders stayed on and did good work, so that everyone was satisfied. Anders had good reason to be pleased with this arrangement, for now there were children always at hand to keep him company. Children who had no parents to provide for them were taken in by the Church. These children lived in the main house with a platoon of nuns.

Not only did Anders entertain these children with his stories, but when they were not in school, he instructed them in the proper care of the gardens. He showed them how to best grow all manner of flowers, but they all learned that the sweet smelling roses were his favorites.

With regret, Anders stopped going to entertain the children from Suzette's old school. It was one thing to leave his work in the middle of the afternoon to run off and tell stories when he was gardening for people who were like family to him; it was quite another thing to take such liberties now that he was employed by a formal institution. He felt obliged to stay at work in the gardens until the day was done, but by then the town's children would long be gone to their homes.

It was difficult to tell the children at the town square he could see them no more. He still had the nuns' orphans to entertain, which was fine for him, but the town children had no one else who would invent stories for them with such love and care. Anders felt sorry for them, but his time was now obliged toward earning his keep.

Instead of going to the town square in the afternoons, Anders went to an open area within his garden in the evenings. This spot was a large, circular park, paved with stones and ringed with benches. Here the small wards of the Church learned to gather around him and listen to his marvelous stories. Word of these meetings spread, and soon some of the children from the town square found their way to the grounds of the religious school as the sun sank low.

One night, some months after the tradition of storytelling in the garden had been established, there came a knock on Anders's cottage door. Anders was not accustomed to receiving visitors, less so after nightfall. He opened the door with great curiosity. Finding one of the nuns standing outside his threshold, he became even more curious, as the nuns were not in the habit of walking the grounds at night.

Anders recognized the nun immediately. It was Sister Clemence, known to the children as Sister Clem. Sister Clem was in charge of all the nuns at the school. She had given Anders instructions a few times and there was a definite air of authority in her demeanor.

Anders bowed slightly. "Welcome, Sister. Please come in. I was just making some tea. Would you have a cup?"

"Thank you, no. I expect my visit will be too brief for that."

"As you wish. Allow me to offer you a seat."

"What I have to say won't take long," she said, taking no interest in sitting, though he led her into the sitting room.

"Of course," he replied. "I can imagine how valuable your time must be."

Sister Clem wasted no more time on niceties. "It has been widely noticed that you have begun a custom of gathering the children in the garden every evening."

Anders nodded. "Yes. I tell them stories. They seem to enjoy it."

"Indeed. Well, I'm afraid we must put a stop to it."

Anders's eyes, jaw, and shoulders dropped all at once. "Stop?"

"Exactly."

Despite the fact that the nun remained standing, Anders backed himself into a chair and sat down abruptly. "But, why?"

Sister Clem remained standing. She spoke downward at him. "To begin with, you are not employed here as a teacher or storyteller. You are employed as a gardener. All who teach here have been instructed to ensure their lessons are according to Scripture. I have oversight of all lessons. Outside the classroom, I have no means of knowing that what is being taught to the children is in accordance with Scripture." Sister Clem squinted. "In fact, I have no guarantee that it is not in opposition to Scripture."

Anders leaned forward. "I admit, I am no expert of Scripture. But I am not trying to be a teacher. I only hope to add a few smiles to the children's days."

The nun's stance remained rigid. "Even so."

"If you fear there is something sinful in my stories, I invite you to come listen with the children. You are always welcome."

The nun crossed her arms. "It is not plain sinfulness I fear in your stories, Mr. Christiansen; rather it is that which appears harmless, but distracts the children from the true nature of their studies. The children have much to learn, and their minds must be focused on what is truly important."

139

"Won't you listen to just one story with the children?" Anders begged. "You'd see it does them no harm."

Sister Clem rocked from one foot to the other. "Even if I had time for that, I'm sure it would make no difference." Impatient to end the discussion, she pressed her argument. "What's more, it's been noticed that children from outside our school have joined in your gatherings, mixing among our students without our supervision. This cannot be allowed. We must not have outside children roaming the grounds in the evenings."

Anders tried to reply but found his throat choked by the mournful prospects Sister Clem laid before him. At last, he found hoarse words. "I will ask the other children to stay away," he said, knowing that even doing this would cause him great sadness.

"I'm afraid the situation has gone beyond that, Mr. Christiansen," she replied.

She stared at him to make certain her point was understood so she could close this unpleasant conversation. She wished him to nod, or to say, in the fewest possible words, that he understood and would obey.

Instead, he said, "Sister, I ask you again to sit and have a cup of tea. There is something I would like to tell you."

Sister Clem was at the point of telling him that she had no more time to devote to this issue, but when he looked her in the eye, she hesitated. There was something in his eyes like the searching gaze of a stray dog. Like a homeless pup, his eyes begged for a morsel, fearful the request would only bring the wrath of a stranger. It was the look of one who would not open himself to such vulnerability, except that the morsel sought was vital to his existence. "Oh, very well," Sister Clem sighed.

When Sister Clem was seated and provided with tea, Anders sat opposite her. He chose his words carefully, allowing himself long pauses that would have embarrassed him in younger days. "You may have noticed that my speech is slower than most," he began.

The nun nodded. "It is deliberate, but there is no harm in that," she said, showing an impatience that contradicted her words.

"When I was younger, I was sometimes called a half-wit because of my speech. It was only children who dared say it to my face. The adults were polite and said these things behind my back."

Sister Clem listened. She was in no mood for a biography, but she knew not how to forestall him without rudely cutting him short.

"It was very upsetting," Anders continued, "more so since I knew it was untrue. Their words made me dislike myself. I knew I was not what they called me, but I could do nothing to disprove them and I hated that about myself."

With reluctance, Sister Clem settled deeper into her chair.

"I felt trapped within myself," Anders explained. "I could not make myself be the man I was meant to be."

Sister Clem sipped her tea. She was thankful for the cup now as it allowed her an excuse to break eye contact with the gardener.

"Along the way, I began telling stories to the schoolchildren. The stories made their eyes light up and they stopped calling me a half-wit. I think the adults may have stopped too. The stories made the children happy, and that gave my life some worth."

The nun caught herself nodding. She quickly took another sip of tea.

"Over the years, Sister, everything and everyone I have loved has left me. All but the children and the stories I tell them. For these two things, I am happy. I don't dislike myself any longer. I am what I am, and that is enough. If I have, here and there, given some children joy, that is the man I was meant to be."

Sister Clem steeled herself against the plea she sensed coming by inching forward in her chair.

"Sister, I am growing old. I have not the needs of a young man, but I still need something. The children and the stories I tell are all I have. They are all I need. Don't take these last things away from me."

Sister Clem stood up to bolster the authority of her words. "You are a most excellent gardener, Mr. Christiansen. You bring an artist's touch to the grounds, as I'm sure you have done for many years. In that, you are a very useful man. Your gardens brighten the lives of all who see them. Take your pleasure in that. There is great reward in the work you do, if you would only accept it. But as far as the children are concerned, I'm afraid that matter has been decided. There must be no more storytelling, and there must be no more outside children milling about in the evenings. I'm sorry, but that is the way it must be."

Anders took a breath as though he would remonstrate with her more, but all at once he decided to keep the words to himself. He pursed his lips, closed his eyes, and nodded a short, resigned nod.

He might have told her the story of how his speech came to be so slow, and what more he had lost beyond fluid words, but he remained silent. He doubted it would sway her, even if he could tell it in a way meaningful to her. Besides, it was a story he had never told before. It was not easy for him to talk about the way he used to be and the event that had changed him. He knew he would tell it awkwardly. He would muddle it and Sister Clem would leave more confused about him, and with her decision about the children more entrenched than ever. He took the tea cup from the nun and let her say goodnight without another word of protest.

CHAPTER 33

The children must have been warned against looking to him for more stories. They did not gather in the garden in the evenings. Some of them passed by him during the day as they went along the grounds. Each child was careful not to speak to him, but they all looked at him with beseeching eyes, as if to say that if he wanted to stop them long enough to whisper a little fairy tale into their ears, they would not at all be annoyed by it.

Anders tried to avoid seeing their eyes when they looked at him. The sadness shown there was too much to bear. Did they think it was his decision to cease telling them stories? Surely, the nuns had told them the truth of the matter. Regardless, it was impossible that the children should believe he had turned his back on them. He might tell the children it was the nuns' fault he did not tell stories anymore, but it would not do to say a word against their guardians.

Anders sunk lower with each passing day. Not inconsequential to his gloom was his feeling that the children were sinking lower as well. Their eyes stopped beseeching and turned down toward the ground as they passed. It was one thing to have to learn the lessons of loss, but to watch the children endure such lessons was torture.

Anders went back to the fountain in the town square when his day's work was done. He hoped he might regain some of his audience of schoolchildren there, but children had dispersed to their homes by this hour.

Anders sat on the fountain wall and watched as the merchants of the place concluded their day's business and left one by one. Some of them cast glances his way, perhaps wondering why he still lingered about the empty streets. Others paid him no more heed than they paid the other familiar sights of the town as they hurried off to their homes.

In the gathering darkness, Anders wandered the streets, watching the town close itself down. Was this the same thing that would happen to him? Would loneliness eventually close him down? He had endured loneliness before, but the children had always been there to carry him past it. Could he get past the loneliness of losing this last great gift? He searched his soul as he wandered, but the answer was not to be found.

It was selfish to think only of his own loss. He must think about the feelings of the children too. Even if he could regain his audience at the town square, the orphans would continue to pass by awkwardly, knowing his presence would no longer reward them with entertaining stories. They would always be reminded that there was a delight right in front of them, but it was not for them to enjoy it.

At length, it occurred to Anders that the children might better live with the loss of their favorite pastime if they were not suffered to see their erstwhile storyteller whenever they walked from one part of the grounds to another. Maybe they had better not see him at all. It was a frightening thought. Anders had lived his entire adult life in this one place. Still, it was an idea that must be considered.

There was a decision to be made, and it was an agonizing one. To leave this place meant turning the world upside down. Beyond these grounds, nothing was certain. There was no home, no work, no one to turn to. How he might sustain himself away from this single place was a mystery to Anders. A decision to leave might mark the end of him.

A decision to stay, and to watch the children mope past him, bound from using his gifts to cheer them, would certainly mark the end of him. It would be a slow and agonizing end, killing his spirit if not his life. The uncertainty of the outside world was to be feared, but this future was to be avoided at all costs.

These thoughts played in Anders's mind one night as he returned from his evening walk along the streets of town. Passing through the gardens, he heard an unusual rustling within the border hedge. Anders stopped to investigate, suspecting some destructive rodent of playing mischief within the carefully sculpted grounds.

As Anders crept toward the hedge, the rustling ceased. He knelt to peer into the darkness, on guard against the attack of a cornered

144

animal. He could see nothing, yet to his ear came the sound of muffled breathing. This seemed odd; Anders had never heard a rodent breathe before. He crept closer.

He spied two small shoes in a gap below the bushes of the hedge. The shoes were scuffed with wear, and more importantly, attached to two small feet. The two small feet were attached to two small legs, and this was the full extent of the connections Anders could see, the small legs disappearing behind the cover of the shrubbery.

Anders sat down beside the hedge. "Hello," he called out softly. "You there, in the hedge. Are you a hedgehog?"

There was no reply. Even the breathing became more quiet.

"Oh, I certainly hope you're not a hedgehog," Anders went on. "This is no place for hedgehogs. There's bound to be trouble for you in that case."

From within the hedge came a whisper. "I'm not a hedgehog."

"That's good news," Anders replied. "I hate to trouble you again, but you're not a hungry hare, come to nibble my flowers, I hope."

"No," returned the whisper from the hedge.

"That is a great relief to me," Anders said. "I've got an idea. Why don't you come out of the hedge. Then, I won't have to keep guessing wrong. I'm a poor guesser, you know. I could guess wrong all night."

The hedge rustled. A hand emerged. Anders took it and gently drew a child from the greenery. Her face was smeared with dirt and scratched by branches. She was one of the orphans.

Before Anders was forbidden to tell his stories to the orphans, he had learned the names of them all. This one was named Greta. She had often been among the first to arrive when the children gathered around Anders. She'd drunk in Anders's stories with her wide eyes as much as with her perked ears. Having once been a child who adored a clever story, Anders could tell which children loved his stories best, and Greta had been affected most deeply by his tales.

Anders would have been taken aback at finding any child hiding in the shrubbery, but he was especially surprised to find such a quiet, timid child as Greta there. "Greta? What are you doing out here in the dark?" he asked.

Though Anders's tone was gentle, Greta merely looked at him in shamefaced silence.

"Don't be afraid, child. You can tell me," Anders assured her.

"I was hiding," Greta whispered.

"Hiding? From whom?"

She couldn't look him in the eye. "From you."

"Me? Why would you need to hide from me?"

"I heard you coming and I thought you were one of the nuns, so I hid."

Anders nodded. "Ah, I see." He made sure to digest this perfectly reasonable answer before he continued. "Now, tell me, why are you out in the shrubbery at night, listening for nuns?"

Now that her fear of being discovered by the nuns had subsided, Greta seemed almost eager to explain herself. "I'm running away," she said with a touch of defiance in her quiet voice.

"Ah yes, running away," Anders repeated, nodding thoughtfully. "That's serious business. Where will you go?"

"I don't know. Anywhere. Just away from here."

"Is there someone to care for you?"

Greta stiffened her shoulders. "I'll look after myself."

"Well. Running away with nowhere to go. You must have some very strong reasons. Do they not give you enough to eat?"

"They give me plenty."

"Do you not have a comfortable place to sleep?"

"My bed is quite comfortable."

"Then what could make you so determined to run away?"

She looked away from his face. "It's you," she said, with none of her former defiance.

"Me? Again, me?" Anders sighed. "You are beginning to make me doubt my own character."

"I'm sorry," Greta whispered, and her voice said she really was.

"What have I done to make you run away?" Anders asked.

"You've reminded me of my grandfather, and made me happy for the first time since he died." She battled impending tears.

"Tell me about your grandfather," Anders said.

"My grandfather raised me. He wasn't often well enough to play games with me, so he told me stories. He told me stories all the time, until he died and they brought me here. At first, I felt all alone. Then, I started to come to hear you tell stories and it was like listening to my grandfather again. I didn't feel so alone anymore, so long as I could listen to your stories. But then, they told us we couldn't listen to your stories anymore, and it was like losing my grandfather all over again."

"And that's why you're running away?"

"It was an awfully mean thing for them to do, even meaner since all of us have to see you working in the gardens every day. We see you, but we know we aren't allowed to hear your stories, no matter how badly we'd like to."

"I'm sure they didn't intend to be mean," Anders explained.

"It doesn't matter. I don't want to have to see you anymore. It just reminds me that now I've lost two grandfathers."

"I wish I could tell you, and all my friends, all the stories you'd like, but the nuns must have a good reason for the rules they make."

Greta looked at him as though she weren't sure about that. "Mean is mean, whether there's a good reason or not," she said.

Anders rested a hand on the girl's head. "Listen to me," he said. "The world is not a place for a girl of your age to be out on her own. If you promise me you won't run away, I promise you won't have to look at an old grandfather who can't tell you any stories anymore. Is that a bargain?"

Greta's breathed out a long breath. It was a relief not to have to run away. "All right."

"Shake on it." He offered his hand and she shook it.

"Now that that's settled, why don't you go back inside and get yourself to bed? And take care the nuns don't catch you."

147

Greta smiled and nodded. Anders walked her to where he could watch her sneak safely back into the house.

As he walked back to his cottage he thought how silly it was for a child to contemplate running away from a place where she was cared for so well. It was foolishness to run away. Maybe it was different for an adult.

CHAPTER 34

He would go. Where he would go, he did not know, but he would go nonetheless. He was a skilled gardener; maybe he could find a new employer. He didn't need much, a roof over him at night and a bite to eat every day. There were no attachments to keep him here. He was free to follow whatever opportunity afforded itself. Even if he found himself degraded to begging for daily bread, it was only he who would be laid low.

He would miss this place. In these gardens he had mastered his trade. In this cottage, he'd formed the daily habits of his lifetime. All around were the memories that composed his character, and in one hallowed spot behind his house lay the remains of a cherished friend. It would not be easy to say goodbye, but he was convinced it must be done.

He arranged for an audience with Sister Clem to inform her of his intentions. At the appointed time, he was welcomed at the door of the main building. This was the house where Suzette's family once lived. He had not been inside it for a long time. Much had changed.

Though the shapes of the rooms were the same, it was a different place. No longer a warm home, it was a place of business, with people constantly flowing through it, but none belonging to it. Though it was warm outside, Anders felt a chill as he came inside. The house was well-maintained, but that was different from being well-cared-for, as it once had been.

Anders was ushered into the very same room where he had met the Minister of the Exchequer for his first formal interview so many years ago. This room was the least changed of all those Anders saw. Once the Minister's place to conduct his business, it was where Sister Clemence guided the business of the entire school now.

Memories crowded his mind as he crossed the room. He recalled how nervous he'd been to address such an important man. He'd barely been able to utter a few words. It occurred to him that he was older

149

now than the Minister had been at that time. This made him remember the man's untimely end. He felt a prick of guilt at this, as he still felt at fault for the Minister's death.

Anders was not nervous today. The years had matured him so that his nerves were subdued by the strength of his resolve. There was only a tinge of sadness at all the changes wrought by the past, and the ones approaching in the future.

Sister Clem's desk was positioned where Gustav's desk once stood. Her desk was not half as ornate as his, but it was nearly as large, at least the books and papers piled high above it made it seem so. There was a sense of presentation in the Minister's office. It had been designed to accommodate visitors more than to serve as a lonely workplace. Sister Clem's office was arranged for one who preferred to work in solitude, without regard to the impression made on visitors.

Sister Clem wasn't in the habit of entertaining visitors. She could hardly see a visitor over the stack of books on her desk. Anders, and the nun who brought him, came right up to the desk, yet Sister Clem took no note of them above the collection of papers that claimed her attention. At last, Anders's companion cleared her throat. "Excuse me, Sister. I believe this gentleman has arranged to speak to you."

Sister Clem was startled out of the reverie of her work. "What? Who?" At last she recognized the gardener. "Ah, Mr. Christiansen. Of course. Pardon me. I lost track of the time." While Anders nodded his understanding, Sister Clem dismissed the nun who had guided him.

"Please take a seat, Mr. Christiansen," Sister Clem said, craning to see around the pile of books. "I believe there is a chair there."

There was none, but Anders found one a short distance away and brought it to the front of the nun's desk. Meanwhile the nun pushed and pulled at books, trying to make a gap through which she could see him. At last, they sat face to face through a makeshift window of bound volumes.

"Now then, Mr. Christiansen," Sister Clem began, "what is it you wished to speak to me about?"

Anders swallowed hard. Now that the time came to announce his decision, he had trouble coming out with it. "There's something I have to tell you," he said.

"That was my assumption," the nun agreed. "What is it? You can see I have much work to do."

"I have come to tell you," Anders paused, taking a long breath, "I will be leaving."

"Leaving? What do you mean *leaving*?"

Anders looked down at his hands as they rested in his lap. "Going away from here, to make my living someplace else."

The nun, who had retained her pencil and remained hovered over her work, as though expecting this interruption to last only a minute or two, set down her pencil and sat up straight. "Where? Where will you go?"

"I don't know." Anders fidgeted his embarrassment. "Somewhere else."

"No one has offered you a place? You are not being enticed away from us?"

Anders shook his head. "No."

The nun stood up. This was not the simple conversation she had planned to conclude from behind a window in her stack of books. She came around to the side of her desk and stood, arms folded, looking down at Anders. She sighed. "Is it because I forbade you to tell your stories to the children? Is that why you feel you must go?"

Anders hesitated. He did not want it to seem as if he were acting out of anger, yet he felt he must tell the truth. "That's at the root of it, I suppose."

The nun shook her head in exasperation and looked up toward the ceiling. "Dear Lord, I try to do my best," she said to the space above her. "Forgive me my failings."

Anders leaned forward. "I didn't mean to upset you, Sister."

The nun ignored the remark. She let her eyes fall down to Anders. "Mr. Christiansen, you are a skilled gardener. I am loathe to lose you."

151

"Thank you, Sister."

"And maybe we won't have to lose you after all."

"Sister?"

The nun let her shoulders relax and her arms fall to her side. She looked like a different person when she did that. "Mr. Christiansen, I am not one prone to doubting my own decisions. But when I do find reason to question them I make every attempt to examine the question fairly."

Anders nodded, wondering if he were expected to say something.

"In the weeks since I told you to cease telling stories," the nun resumed, "we have been plagued by the most morose atmosphere. The children mope around the school as if they have nothing but misery to expect. They are inattentive in class. They are argumentative with each other. They find joy in nothing. It is as if all the light has gone out of their lives."

"You see, I am being fair," the nun interrupted herself. "I don't have to tell you this, but I am telling you anyway, out of fairness."

"Of course, Sister," Anders answered, still not sure exactly what the nun was building toward.

"We've tried time and again to find the source of this dark cloud that overhangs the children. Whenever we get a glimpse of it, it always has the look of your stories behind it."

Anders stiffened at what sounded like an accusation. "I assure you, Sister, I would never do anything to make the children unhappy."

"No, no, Mr. Christiansen. I quite understand that if you played any role in upsetting the children, it was purely unintentional. What I mean to say is the children grew so fond of hearing your stories; it was a great disappointment to them when they could hear them no more."

Anders made no reply. He was occupied with trying to determine if the nun had absolved him of all of the blame for the children's sour moods or only part of it.

"Of course, we knew it would be disappointing to them, but we did not expect it to have such a profound effect. It is quite disturbing."

"It disturbs me as well," Anders replied, having given up trying to determine to what degree she held him responsible for the low morale of the children.

"Mr. Christiansen, I have been turning this issue over in my mind for some time, and your presence here has decided me. I'm not a cruel person. I didn't forbid you to tell the children stories because I wished to bleed them of joy. I was merely trying to protect them."

Anders remained silent, wondering who would need be protected from him.

"Yes, we must all learn to live humbly in this earthly existence, but we need not be miserable," the nun went on. "We gain nothing by having children moping around day and night." She clenched her teeth as though the words caused her agony. "I am now prepared to admit I was wrong. I had no proof that your stories harmed the children, but there is some evidence that they may help them. I give you permission to resume telling your stories."

Anders leapt from his chair. His impulse was to rush forward and wrap Sister Clemence in a grateful embrace, but the Sister's demeanor knocked down this idea before he could take a single step toward her. "Thank you, Sister! You've made me so happy! I promise, you won't regret it."

Sister Clem had no faculty for receiving gratitude. Her demeanor remained businesslike. "Thank the children," she said. "They are the ones who have done you the favor."

"Yes. The children. Of course," said Anders in the awkward way of one attempting to atone for having offered unwelcomed gratitude.

Sister Clem spied another nun near the doorway and called her in. "Mr. Christiansen, meet Sister Katrine. She will sit among the children while you tell them your stories. She is to be my eyes and ears, making sure your stories are proper and right for the children to hear."

Anders bowed to Sister Katrine. She was a young woman, not many years removed from childhood herself. Perhaps the confusion written across her face at this unexpected assignment made her look

153

more youthful. Anders welcomed her presence among the children. "I look forward to her joining us," he said.

"May I assume this means you have given up your idea of leaving us?" Sister Clem asked.

"Leave? Who would ever leave such a wonderful home as this?" a giddy Anders responded.

"Very well. I shall consider this matter settled. You are excused."

A less conscientious man would have left without questioning his success. Anders asked the final question that rose to his mind. "The children from the town, if they should wish to join in again?"

"I had quite forgotten about them," the nun admitted. "I think it best they be discouraged from congregating on the property."

Anders shoulders drooped. He had given back part of his victory.

"Can you give them their own stories, at their own time?" Sister Clem asked.

"I used to go to them in the afternoons in the town square."

"Why did you stop?"

"When I began working for the Church, I thought it would be dishonest of me to give part of my work day to other causes."

The nun almost smiled. "Take an hour in the afternoons and give the town's children their stories. My faith in God's mercy toward our gardens is strong. He will not let them fall to ruin."

Anders beamed. "Yes, Sister, just as you wish!"

"Now," the nun concluded, "with your permission, may I put this issue behind me?"

"Entirely."

Chapter 35

For decades Anders had shared the greatest gift he possessed with the children. Now, they gave him the greatest gift for which he could have wished. He'd never have devised an argument persuasive enough to change Sister Clem's mind. They did so merely by demonstrating the difference a daily gift from the heart made to all of their lives. The generosity of his giving had come back around to him again.

His audience of orphans returned to him in the garden clearing. They looked up at him with bright smiles like rising suns, even as the real sun drifted downward toward the horizon. He looked back at them with a new, shinier gleam in his eyes, for he had finally found someone he loved who proved they would never leave him. Each child might grow to adulthood and go out into the world, but the group, the children, would always come to share the gifts he offered them.

At the back of the group sat Sister Katrine. At first, she stood out awkwardly, unsure of her place and of what her superior expected her to accomplish by being there. Within days, she became as comfortable as the children, smiling and laughing at the tales, and likely forgetting she had been sent there for any other purpose than to be entertained.

Anders's audience in town took longer to regain. Having grown unused to seeing him, they had given up looking. It was like starting all over again, as in Suzette's day. In ones and twos they rediscovered him, until the number of children gathered around the fountain finally equaled what it had been at its peak.

Anders did his best to tell both groups of children the same story every day, so that neither would be tempted to mingle with the other at a place where they should not have been. He was mostly successful, but on occasion he let his guard slip with the orphans. He cherished the gift they had given him, and sometimes he felt compelled to tell them a little extra something.

Then, he would tell the remarkable story of how a mere pup of a stray dog once saved a drowning man's life. He did not tell them of the many other times she had kept the man from drowning in the darkness within himself, although he knew those stories just as well. This story made the children especially thoughtful. Maybe they knew a similar story, about a group of poor, parentless children who had prevented a solitary man from spinning adrift into the wide world by providing him a home where he could always be happy.

Though that solitary man was now hardly more than 50 years old, his hair had turned gray. Gardening kept him in the sun through the long summer days, making his face appear weathered and older than its years. The children thought him much older than his actual age.

Suzette wrote to tell him her eldest son, Erik, would be coming to attend the university. She asked Anders to look out for him and keep him away from any trouble. It was the sort of request a mother makes, never thinking there will be any need of it. Anders, in his devotion to Suzette, took the request to heart, as though it were the most important of his responsibilities.

When Erik began at the university, Anders put himself at Erik's service. Erik was polite, but he felt no need of special attention. After some pleasantries were exchanged, Anders left him alone. Anders did not call again, knowing that any young man in Erik's position would be proud of his new independence. Further intrusion could well make the youth resentful.

Instead, Anders looked after him in passing. The young men of the university often gathered at various meeting places in the evenings. Since Anders found it agreeable to walk about the town at night, he used the opportunity to keep a distant watch over Erik, in fulfillment of Suzette's request.

For a long time, there was no need for Anders to be more than a casual observer of Erik's life. The young man led a perfectly normal existence, facing nothing more dangerous than the exams at the end of the term. Happy and healthy, he'd begun courting a young lady, which certainly did nothing to hinder his contentment.

One evening, everything changed. Anders found Erik and some

of his classmates in an excited huddle outside one of their gathering places. Erik was at the center of the huddle.

Anders hid his face as best he could, and came near the group, lingering as long as he dared without attracting their attention. The bits of their excited talk he overheard filled his heart with fear. They spoke of a duel between Erik and one Captain Heidler. Anders could not tell the exact cause of the dispute, but it sounded as if it had to do with the young lady Erik was courting.

Only one of Erik's companions attempted to dissuade him from the duel. "It's utter madness to duel with Heidler," this solitary voice of reason pleaded. "He is said to be an excellent marksman. Have you ever so much as held a pistol in your hand?"

"It can't be helped," Erik replied. "It's a matter of honor."

"You'll take honor to your grave," his sensible friend warned. "And if, by some miracle, you escape death, your honor will send you to prison. Dueling has been outlawed for decades. Heidler is a foreign diplomat. His country will protect him from the law. Who will keep you out of prison?"

"Enough lecturing," Erik bristled. "I have accepted his terms, and I am a man of my word. I will not back down."

Anders's heart sank. He knew he must prevent this duel, but his mind reeled as he tried to think how to do it. He could not let Suzette's child be killed. His inaction had let her father be killed; he would not remain idle and let harm befall her son. Yet, what could he do? If Erik would not listen to reason from one of his peers, why would he listen to an old man he barely knew?

Dark hopelessness spread across Anders's mind, making it harder for him to construct a solution to this problem. He feared he would fall down unconscious in the middle of the street from despair.

The darkness was on the verge of overwhelming him when Erik announced the young man who would be his second in the duel. At this, Anders began to see the elusive light shining under the door in his mind.

157

The group of students began to break up. Young men walked off in different directions. The light grew brighter in Anders's mind. He hurried to overtake one of the students.

Anders put his hand on the shoulder of the student as he overtook him. The young man spun around to confront the intrusion. "What's this? Who are you?" he asked.

"I'm a friend," Anders replied.

"How very odd. I don't recollect your face."

"Listen," Anders demanded. "You are to be Erik's second."

The student frowned. "How do you know that?"

Anders ignored the question. "Tell me. Where is this duel to take place? And when?"

"What business is it of yours? Go away, old man." The student started to walk away, but Anders stopped him.

"Dueling is against the law," Anders warned. "Tell me where and when, or I will report you to the police."

The youth was silent. He stared at Anders's face, not knowing what to make of the threat.

"Is it worth prison to you to see your friend die?" Anders asked.

The student's face softened. He told Anders the name of the field where the duel was to take place. "We meet there at eight, tomorrow morning."

"How will Erik get there?" Anders asked.

"I suppose he will hire a cab, the same as myself."

"You did right to tell me," Anders said. "Now go home to bed. Sleep late in the morning. If I see your face tomorrow, you'll answer to the police."

The student knit his brow. "Who *are* you?" he asked.

But Anders was already walking away.

CHAPTER 36

Anders did not sleep that night. Instead he paced back and forth across the front room of his cottage, running his plan through his mind over and over again, and praying it would succeed.

At dawn, he took a small box out of the cupboard. Inside the box was all the money he had. He had been paid a small stipend every year for his gardening work. Being a man of simple tastes, he had not much use for money, so he had been able to save a little sum over time. He put the money into his pocket. Then he got from his closet a long coat with a high collar and a winter hat. He put on these clothes and went out.

His destination was the headquarters of the police. He did not tell the police anything about the young man who was to be Erik's second in the duel. He only told them to expect him to deliver a man into their custody within the next hour or two.

Then he walked in the direction of Erik's lodgings. On the way he found a cabman driving an empty coach along the boulevard. Anders waved his hand to hail the cab.

The cab stopped beside him, but Anders did not get in. Instead, he looked up at the driver and said, "I want to rent your cab for the morning."

The driver nodded. "All right. Get in."

"No," Anders explained. "I don't want to hire you to drive me. I want to rent your whole rig. I want to drive myself."

The cab man nodded toward a side street. "You can rent a rig at the livery."

"No," Anders protested. "I must have a cab." Before the driver could say another word, Anders pulled his money from his pocket and extended it toward the man. "I will pay you a fair price."

The cab man's eyes widened. He could see at a glance that it was more money than he could make driving his cab in a week. "You want it just for the morning?" he asked.

159

A minute later, Anders drove the cab toward Erik's residence. As he drove, he put up the collar of his coat and pulled his hat down so his eyes peeked out below it. Just short of Erik's home, he stopped. He got down and put on a show of tending to his horse. All the while, he watched Erik's door.

At length, the door opened. Much to Anders's relief, Erik stepped out. He hadn't missed him. Anders climbed up into the driver's seat and turned the horse so he could drive the cab toward Erik. His heart beat fast as he attempted to make the cab conspicuous to Erik without drawing the young man's attention to himself.

Erik saw the cab and hailed it. Anders thanked his good luck and reined in the horse. Erik stepped into the coach and told the driver his destination. Anders nodded and grunted without turning toward his passenger. He started the horse moving again.

In spite of the instructions his passenger had given, Anders drove toward the police headquarters. At first, the passenger failed to notice the detour. Anders prayed he wouldn't pay attention until they reached their destination.

Anders's prayer was not answered. At last, the passenger leaned forward. "Driver, this is not the route to my destination."

Anders raised a hand to his ear, pretending he couldn't hear what the passenger said. He must buy a moment to think. He had only that moment to save his plan, and his mind had gone blank.

"I say, this is not the correct route," the passenger shouted.

There was no more time to think. Anders's plan was at the brink of failure. Then, from out of the light that shone under the door in his mind, words came. "This route avoids traffic," Anders replied over his shoulder, making his voice sound gruff. "It will save time in the end." The passenger was mollified with this, and they continued as they'd been going.

At last, they came to the police headquarters. A constable waited out front, which was a great relief to Anders. He pulled the horse to a stop.

160

"What is this? Why do we stop here?" Erik asked.

The constable stepped forward. "Young man, please do me the favor of stepping down from the coach."

"What is the meaning of this?" Erik demanded.

"Off to fight a duel this fine morning?" the constable asked. "A man your age should not be in such a hurry to throw his life away."

Erik considered himself a man of honor. He would not lie to save himself. "How? How could you know?"

The constable took hold of his arm and helped him down. "Every man should be so lucky to have such a good friend as you have here." The constable nodded toward the driver.

Anders wished the constable had not pointed him out. Having been identified as the informant, there was little hope of maintaining his disguise.

Erik looked more carefully and quickly recognized him. "You? You!" Erik shouted. "How could you do this to me? I'll never forgive you!"

The words stung, but Anders faced them. "I did it for the sake of your mother's heart," he said.

The constable addressed Anders. "As I told you this morning, it is not a crime to *intend* to fight a duel, only to actually fight one. We'll hold him here today for his own safety and keep an eye on him for a few days."

"He is a good young man, from a good family," Anders told the officer. "I beg you, treat him kindly."

The constable grinned. "The worst he'll suffer today is boredom."

"Thank you." Anders faced front and started the horse at a slow walk while the officer escorted Erik into the building. When he was sure he was out of sight, he urged the horse into a trot. This cab would go to the field where Erik wanted it to go, but it would do so without him.

So far Anders had done well, but there remained much to do. He had postponed the duel for a day or two, but there was no guarantee it

161

wouldn't still happen once the police lowered their guard. The only permanent solution was to satisfy Captain Heidler that the issue was settled. If this man were as prideful as Erik, of which there could be little doubt, he would not let the issue drop merely because Erik had been detained for a time by the police. Consequently, there must be a duel today, but Erik would be nowhere near it.

Anders sped his cab toward the field. When he arrived, three men were waiting. Anders was happy to see that Erik's second had heeded good advice and stayed away. Anders stepped down from the cab and approached the three men.

Two of the men wore splendid military uniforms. The third was dressed in the suit of a professional man, with a vest and top hat. They stared at Anders as he approached them. They might have expected no one to show up this morning, but they didn't expect the arrival of such a man as this.

When he had attained a comfortable speaking distance, Anders asked, "Which is Captain Heidler?"

One of the military men wore muttonchop whiskers. He stepped forward. "I am Captain Heidler. Who are you? Where is that upstart boy? Has he come to his senses and sent his apology?"

"He is detained by the police. I am his second."

Captain Heidler burst with laughter. "You? You are his second?" The other man in uniform joined in the laughter. The professional man frowned.

Anders stood firm. "Yes. I am his second. I am prepared to take his place."

Captain Heidler stopped laughing. "Nonsense," he roared. "I will not shoot an old man."

"You must," Anders insisted. "Your honor demands it."

"Bah!" Heidler spit. "I will wait for the impudent young pup to disentangle himself from the police. He and I will meet another day. Go home, old man."

Anders did not budge. "The police are watching him. Whenever

162

he comes to meet you, the police will come with him. The duel will be stopped."

Heidler's comrade stepped forward and spoke quietly to him. "If the police were to come, it would be embarrassing. Imagine the stain it would leave on our government to have one of their emissaries caught flouting the laws of his host country."

Heidler stomped his boot into the ground. His lips curled into a snarl as he realized the wisdom of his comrade's words. "Very well, old man," he hissed. "If it pleases you to be shot today, I will shoot you."

Heidler nodded to the man in the vest and top hat. "Mr. Olsen, we will proceed," he said.

Mr. Olsen frowned. "This is highly irregular," he said. "You will gain nothing by shooting an old man."

"Mr. Olsen, a duel has been declared, and a duel must be fought. This change in circumstance is as unpleasant to me as it is to you." He looked with disgust at Anders as he said this. "Nonetheless, a point of honor is a point of honor. Let us conclude this unpleasant business as quickly as we can."

Mr. Olsen shuffled to the carriage that had brought him, shaking his head as he went. From the carriage he retrieved a polished wooden chest. He motioned for the combatants to come near as he opened the chest. Inside, cushioned in a velvet lining, were two dueling pistols. Mr. Olsen asked Anders to choose one of them.

It was of little consequence to Anders which pistol he used. He chose the one nearest him. Heidler immediately picked up the other. They handed the pistols to Mr. Olsen and waited while he loaded each with powder and ball.

When he was done with the pistols, Mr. Olsen handed them back to their respective users. Frowning more than ever, he bade them stand back to back. When they were thus arranged, he instructed them. "I will count ten. On each count, you will both take one pace forward. At ten you will stop. I will then command, 'Turn.' At that command you may turn and fire at will. Is this understood?" He looked at Anders as he asked this question.

"It is," Anders replied. Heidler said nothing.

Mr. Olsen sighed. "Then may God have mercy on you both." He backed away to a place of safety.

Having reached a safe distance, Mr. Olsen addressed them again. "Gentlemen, you may now prepare your pistols for firing." Anders looked over his shoulder and saw that Heidler pulled back the hammer of his pistol so that it would fire at the squeeze of the trigger. Anders prepared his weapon in the same manner.

"Now we begin," Mr. Olsen shouted. "One."

Each of the combatants took his first step.

"Two."

Anders took another step. He could hear Heidler do likewise.

"Three."

Anders didn't listen for Heidler's step. His only concern was that he should take care to fully abide by the rules, leaving no excuse for a repeat duel involving Erik.

"Four."

Anders took another obedient step. He had no sense of Heidler's presence anymore.

"Five."

Another step. The sun was shining. Birds chirped in the trees. The air was crisp and clear. What a glorious last morning it was.

"Six."

Step. Anders thought of Suzette. He hardly remembered the pistol in his hand.

"Seven."

Step. A glorious morning and thoughts of a dear one, what more could a man want?

"Eight."

Step. Suzette would keep her beloved son. It felt satisfying to be making amends for his role in the death of her father. This restitution was more than enough to make it all worth it.

"Nine."

Step. She would welcome her son with a warm hug. Everything would be right in the world.

"Ten."

One last step. Anders smiled. Peace and happiness to those most beloved. That was a happy man's legacy.

"Turn!"

Anders turned with the careless leisure of a satisfied man. He seemed almost surprised to find a man in a military uniform pointing a pistol at him. Perhaps he was surprised that the man had not yet fired.

Anders glanced down at his own hand, hanging at his side. That there should be a pistol in that hand might have been the biggest surprise of all. Anders raised the pistol, but only so that it was pointed at the ground a little ways ahead of him. He tensed as he squeezed the trigger. With a flash of smoke, the pistol discharged its ball harmlessly into the earth. Anders tossed the pistol to the side.

He gazed across the field at Captain Heidler and patiently waited for death.

Heidler stared down the barrel of his own pistol at Anders. Why he took so much time to fire was a mystery. Anders was certainly an easy target for his famed marksmanship at this distance. It seemed like his arm must drop from fatigue if he waited much longer.

Anders stood straight and waited. If Heidler wished to make him suffer for a while, he supposed that must be the man's right, by the rules of this peculiar game. The end would come soon enough.

At last Heidler shouted an oath. Anders saw the smoke and felt something whiz past his head. A fraction of a second later, he heard the sound of the discharge, and felt a stinging in his earlobe.

In the next second, Heidler was shouting angry words at him. "I did not give you what you deserved, old man," Heidler yelled. "But maybe the scar on your ear will remind you in the future to stay out of other men's affairs." He stomped over to Mr. Olsen and thrust his empty pistol at that man, but he was not done admonishing Anders. "This affair is over. Your young friend may rest easy in his cowardice. But tell him this: if he should ever cross me again, neither the police nor his pitiful old grandfather will have the power to save him."

Heidler stalked to his carriage and made a show of waiting for his companions. Mr. Olsen came to collect Anders's pistol. "Do you need assistance?" he asked as he drew near.

Anders shook his head. "I'm not much hurt," he said, wiping the blood from his earlobe. "It's merely a reminder."

Mr. Olsen gave him a piece of cloth to use as a bandage. Then he hurried back to join Heidler and the other soldier in their carriage. The three of them drove off at a trot.

Anders wrapped the cloth around his ear. "I fought in a duel today," he told himself. Then he huffed at the ridiculous idea and went to return the cab to its owner.

Chapter 37

That night, someone came banging at Anders's door. He was not completely surprised by this, nor was he wholly prepared for it. Just the same, he opened the door and invited Erik into his home.

Erik didn't answer the invitation. "How dare you meddle in my affairs?" he demanded as he marched into Anders's front room. "What right have you?"

"Please make yourself comfortable," Anders replied, pointing to a soft chair. "Will you have some tea with me? I like to take a cup of tea in the evenings."

"I don't want any tea," Erik growled. "I want you out of my life for good."

"I see." Anders nodded. "Won't you at least have a seat? Our visit will be more comfortable sitting down."

Erik threw himself into the chair. "There. Now will you tell me why you have ruined my life?"

Anders sat down opposite the young man. "Ruined?" he asked.

"Yes, ruined. Heidler has every right to denounce me as a coward for missing our appointment this morning. For someone of my place to be branded a coward is to have his life ruined."

"Oh no, you don't understand," Anders insisted. "Heidler has no right to say such things. He received his satisfaction. Honor," he made a face as he said the word, "was served all around."

Erik grimaced. "How can that be? I failed to present myself at the appointed time." He thought for a moment. "Did my second fight? Is it possible?"

Anders shrugged. "I suppose you could say that."

"My friend Olaf stood in my place?"

"Well, maybe not Olaf, but someone who made an equally fine target."

"What? Who?" Erik's eyes narrowed. "What happened to your ear?"

167

"It's nothing," Anders assured him. "Just a little reminder of how foolish boys can be."

"How did you get this little reminder?"

"I stood in the right place to be reminded."

The gathering light exploded into Erik's eyes. "You? You faced Heidler?"

Anders said nothing, and thus said everything.

Erik cast his eyes at the floor. "How humiliating!" he groaned.

"The only man who is never humiliated is a dead one," Anders told him. "That is my little reminder to *you*."

"Dead? Why, I should have a little nick on my ear, like you have, and my honor would be held high, instead of trampled as it is now."

Anders's expression hardened. "Heidler nicked my ear because he aimed there. He could have killed me if he chose to. He would have killed you."

"Even so, my honor would be preserved."

"Your *life* is preserved. You are young, and you are alive."

"There is more to life than that."

"There is nothing more you need. Youth needs only life; that's all."

"Enough!" Erik exploded. "Clearly you are too simple-minded to understand. I'll waste no more time on you." He rose and marched for the door. Anders followed a step behind. At the door, Erik turned to Anders. "You're a brave man, so I will let this unpleasantness between us drop. You'll hear no more from me." He scowled. "But I will never forgive you for what you did today."

"I ask no forgiveness," Anders replied. "I ask only that you stay clear of this Heidler fellow."

"I will be the master of my own actions," Erik declared.

Anders made his face as soft as he could. "I ask this in the name of your dear mother," he said.

Erik, at the point of slamming the door behind him, paused. Some of the defiance drained from his countenance. He went out and closed the door softly behind him.

Anders worried that Erik's pride would get the better of him. He feared Erik would not keep away from Heidler, and in consequence, would allow himself to be destroyed by his foolish desire to preserve his honor.

Anders continued to do his best to watch over the young man, but that was more difficult now. Having stepped into the youth's life once, it was not easy to hover near him without attracting his notice. Anders did what he could to keep watch, and prayed it would not be necessary to step into Erik's life again.

To Anders's great relief, Erik did not put himself in danger again while at the university. Perhaps he didn't have the opportunity to cross paths with the likes of Captain Heidler. Perhaps his keen interest in his own honor was overtaken by an interest in some other subject. Maybe he had been swayed by Anders's plea to think of his mother's feelings. In any event, Erik earned his degree and went to live where he could best apply his education without any more trouble.

All the while, Anders exchanged an occasional letter to Suzette, as had been his habit for years past. Though he mentioned Erik in each letter, he never wrote a word about the affair with Captain Heidler. It was the type of near miss that perhaps it was best for a mother to not have to contemplate.

CHAPTER 38

Every evening during the next five years, Sister Katrine sat with the children to hear the day's story. Though the resemblance between the children and herself diminished, she still smiled at the charm of the tales along with the rest. If there were a sad part, her countenance fell every bit as downcast as that of the smallest child.

She conjured up these reactions to show empathy to the children. This could be the only reason. Anders had long since concluded that his creative abilities could not touch the emotions of an adult in such a way. Sister Katrine must be pretending these feelings for the benefit of the children. For this kindness, Anders grew to like her.

At the end of each story, as the children flew away to their beds, Anders paid Sister Katrine the courtesy of wishing her a good evening and exchanging a few pleasantries. He had never been so forward as to ask about the special assignment Sister Clem had given her. Perhaps it would be viewed as inappropriate for him to make such inquiries.

At last, five years' association with Sister Katrine made him bold. "After all this time, what do you report to Sister Clem of my stories?" he asked her.

She first seemed confused by the question. Then she laughed and answered, "Nothing. Nothing at all."

"Nothing?"

"Of course not. I haven't spoken of this to Sister Clem in years. I doubt she knows I still come here to listen. She absolved me of the responsibility within a few weeks of beginning."

Anders stared at her in amazement. "You're not required to come here? Then why have you come for all this time?"

"Because I like to. Sister Clem says I have too much of the child in me still, and maybe she's right. Your stories are most often the best part of my day."

Anders's jaw fell. He'd never imagined his stories could capture the interest of grown persons.

"You don't mind that I still come, do you?" she asked.

Anders shook his head, rousing his tongue. "No. Of course not. It's an honor for me to welcome you."

"Good. Because I'd hate to miss a minute of it." She paused and grew thoughtful. "What did you think I was telling Sister Clem about you?"

Anders shrugged. "That I was a harmless old man who only told silly stories?"

"Well, if she ever asks, that's precisely what I shall tell her. And then I'll tell her that a harmless old man who only tells silly stories is exactly what the world needs. Good night, Mr. Christiansen."

Anders smiled with satisfaction. "Good night, Sister."

Anders was still mulling Sister Katrine's words when he heard a soft knock at his cottage door. Opening the door, Anders immediately recognized his visitor. Erik's face displayed greater maturity, but his features had not changed since his days at the university.

This visit was quite unexpected, especially after the result of his last visit. Anders was pleased nonetheless. He quickly ushered Erik into his house. "Would you like some tea?" he asked. "I like to take a cup of tea in the evenings."

Erik smiled. "I would like that very much."

After they were seated with their tea, Erik began. "I am in town on business. I thought it would be a fine opportunity to call on you."

"It is very kind of you to think of me. Very kind indeed," Anders replied.

"I especially wanted to speak to you because I wanted to tell you I am getting married next month."

"Splendid! What wonderful news!" Anders leaned forward and shook his hand. "You have my fullest congratulations."

"I also wanted to apologize for the things I said when I was last here."

Anders waved his hands. "No. That's not necessary."

"I'm afraid it's completely necessary," Erik insisted. "You should

171

know how sorry I am, and also how grateful I am to you for what you did for me."

"It was nothing," Anders said.

"Nothing?" Erik said with a chuckle at Anders's humility. "It was everything. Today, I am in love and happy as a lark. I would not be here at all if not for you."

"Let us speak no more about it," Anders insisted. "Tell me about your bride. Is she the same one you doted on in your university days?"

Erik let out a greater chuckle. "Dear Lord, no! That's the tragedy you helped me avoid. She and I parted years ago, even before I'd left the university. We were destined to part. Yet, I nearly threw my life away for the love of her. And I didn't even know what love was. I was such a young fool. When I think back to what might have happened, indeed, what would have happened, if not for you, it sends a shiver down my spine."

Anders smiled, but kept silent.

"My God!" Erik exclaimed. "And then I had the gall to come here and insult you when I should have been on my knees thanking you. I said I would never forgive you for what you had done. Were more ungrateful words ever spoken? Now, I only hope you can forgive *me*. As someone who could not be happier with my life, I cannot express the full measure of my gratitude."

"Consider it expressed," Anders said.

"You are as good a friend to me as you have been to my mother."

They talked late into the night. Anders was always eager for news of Suzette and her family. Erik invited Anders to his wedding, and Anders assured him he would not miss the happy event. At last they shook hands and parted.

Anders went to sleep happy. It felt good to be forgiven, even if he'd done nothing for which he needed forgiveness. Erik profited by the act of forgiving. It was a weight off the young man's conscience and a barrier removed from between them. Life is so much an easier road to travel without weights or barriers.

CHAPTER 39

Anders attended Erik's wedding, and the weddings of Suzette's other children as well. These occasions, when he got to visit Suzette and her family, were treasured moments, more so because of the speed with which they came and went. They were the blinks of an eye that made up a one-thousandth part of the blink of an eye that was the next 10 years.

Anders had looked like an old man for many years, but now he felt himself an old man. Aches in his bones hindered his movements to match what slowness remained in his speech. His gardening was more deliberate, but done with the same care as ever. The chores requiring a young man's strength he could no longer do. An assistant helped him with the heavy toils so he could save his strength for the delicate work among the buds and the blossoms.

He suffered from pains in his chest. At first, he made no mention of this trouble, not wishing to bother others with his infirmities. When the pain became too intense to hide, he submitted to examination by a doctor.

The doctor gave him medicine. "This will help ease the pain," the doctor told him. "I am sorry to say I can do nothing to affect the cause of the pain. Your heart is growing weak, and there is nothing to be done about it. Take your medicine and don't exert yourself, and you will go far toward getting the most out of what strength remains."

Anders thanked the doctor for his trouble, gave him a cup of tea, and immediately turned the conversation to happier topics. He would take his medicine exactly as instructed, but he would not spend time worrying over things there was nothing to be done about. There were too many more important things to occupy him, like sitting among the children and telling them stories.

His fairy tales did not suffer from the passing of time. Though age did nothing to brighten the elusive light in his mind, it did nothing to dim it. It was as it had been for so many years; it dawned for him when it was time to make something from nothing, and melted away after that something had been created. It found him and left him as it always had: a gardener with a story for the children.

Though Anders had no children of his own, he counted many as his grandchildren. The orphans were his special ones. Their joys were his joys, and everything of concern to them, no matter how childish or insignificant, was of concern to him. "None of you are ever alone in the world," he would assure them, "because you all have a grandfather in me."

Children came to the school, grew to adulthood, and left for the big world. He loved them all, and he was sad that some of them had to go at the end of each year. Yet the new children who took their places brought fresh joys. These joys found their way into the stories Anders told. Over the years, the stories lost much of the darkness Anders's youthful trials and tribulations had first brought to them. They ended more happily, and hopefully. Yet, not every story ended with roses and candy canes.

There were still times, late in the evenings, when Anders was left alone to contemplate his history, during which the sadness of expired wishes fell over him. He thought of the old manuscript that had turned to ashes long before he had thrown it into the fire. He remembered all the people who had invested their faith in him and his promise, and had gone to the grave unrewarded for it.

He recalled all the dreams he had dreamt about making a life with Suzette, those many years ago, before such dreams blew away on the breeze like wisps of smoke. Of course, she had made the right choice. He couldn't have given her the life she deserved. There was comfort in this conclusion. Things had worked out for the best, and one cannot long harbor regrets for things that have worked out for the best.

But he could not have loved her more.

"Dreams," he would say to himself. "Only just dreams." Dreams, like stories, sometimes end with just a little tinge of regret.

Anders felt tired quite often now. Some days, an entire side of his body felt numb, as if it were merely some baggage, not really part of him. He suffered spells of forgetfulness, when he could not remember what things he had done a few moments before. Time was getting the better of him. He saw this every morning in the mirror, and he felt it in his bones every night when he lay down to sleep.

One evening, as the children gathered in the garden, waiting for him to tell a story, something wonderful happened. The light peeking out underneath that dark door within Anders's mind grew brighter than it ever had before. As had often happened at moments like this, Anders could see himself sitting at his father's knee within that light.

So many times before, his father, seen within this light, asked him to tell a story. This time, his father in the light asked him to tell *the* story. It was a difference of only one small word, but that word meant everything. Anders beamed at the children gathered around him and told them the story of a housefly in autumn. It went like this.

"Many years ago, in a town very much like our own, there stood a confectioner's shop. The confectioner was very skilled at his trade. He made all manner of candies to satisfy the many children and adults in the community who owned a sweet tooth.

"He would shape his confections into the forms of many everyday things, like houses and animals. But he was most famous for the sweet figurines he molded into the shapes of people.

"One day he made a sugar statuette of a beautiful young woman. It was the most delicate, perfect creation he'd ever accomplished, and he was suitably proud of his masterpiece. He put it on display in the shop's front window, where all the passersby would be sure to see his most brilliant work of art.

"And the people did see it. Such a work of beauty was hardly to be missed. It was such a rare exposition of skill that no one spoke to the confectioner without congratulating him on his exemplary work of craftsmanship.

"The figurine was so beautiful and was made from such sweet ingredients that some people could not resist the desire to want to eat it up. They offered to buy the figurine, but the confectioner, smitten with his own work, refused, even though some of the offers were quite generous.

"As the days went by, some people became determined to have the sweet, little woman. Their offers to the confectioner became more substantial. The confectioner was not a rich man, and though he had once been determined to never part with her, he now said to himself, 'Well, if they offer such a rich price, am I a fool not to take it? Can I not make another figurine?' He thought he should consider selling her before interest in buying her faded.

"At this time it was autumn. This was the confectioner's favorite season because it brought him relief from the houseflies. In summer, he must always be on his guard against the flies, because they have a weakness for sweets, just as people do, but people do not like to share their sweets with insects. So the confectioner kept busy all summer chasing flies from his shop, for there was nothing so bad for business as houseflies.

"Now, the confectioner could relax, for the houseflies were gone. That is to say, all but one were gone. This last housefly of autumn did not attract much attention to himself, because he was slow and stiff, and in consequence, he stayed still and did not buzz around the shop very often.

"Like the people of the town, the housefly had also fallen in love with the sugar figurine. He loved her more than anything in the world. He wanted nothing more than to be with her always, but this he could not do. The confectioner guarded his figurine so jealously that it was quite a great danger for the housefly to even buzz around near her. He moved too slowly to avoid being swatted down by the confectioner.

"At first, the housefly contented himself with loving the figurine from afar. 'As long as I can look upon her every day, even though it gives me no chance to win her love, I will be happy,' he told himself.

"But then the housefly heard the confectioner talking to himself as he decided to sell the figurine. 'This changes matters,' the housefly told himself. 'I don't know how I would live without her. From now on, I must be more active in regard to her.' In this way the housefly convinced himself he must risk his own safety for his love.

"The housefly knew people would be less willing to buy a sweet treat if they saw a housefly buzzing around it. And so he decided he would, even at the risk of his own life, buzz around the figurine in the window and do his best to dissuade customers from wanting to eat her up.

"And the housefly did exactly that. Whenever he saw someone looking through the window, he buzzed around her as conspicuously as he could. At this, the people outside the glass would frown. 'I don't want what the flies have left,' they would say, and then they would move on.

"Now, the beautiful figurine also had overheard the confectioner talk about selling her. She certainly did not want to be sold and eaten up. Does anyone? No. She wanted to stay right there in her window and look out at the wide world and enjoy watching all the different people passing by.

"The figurine saw that the housefly was trying to protect her, and she was grateful to him. 'You are such a wonderful friend to me. If not for you, I would certainly have been eaten up by some hungry child with rich parents by now. What can I do to repay you?' she asked.

"The fly was too shy to ask for her love, so he bided his time and said merely, 'Just stay as sweet and beautiful as you are, and let me buzz around you and be your friend. I know I am slow and clumsy, but I will buzz here for you always if you will only say that you are my dear friend and that you enjoy my company.' The figurine assured him that she was his dear friend and she treasured his company, which made him buzz all the more happily.

"But the figurine and the people outside couldn't see the housefly buzzing in the window without the confectioner seeing him too. The confectioner became very cross when he saw the housefly buzzing, for he believed he was done with such troublesome creatures for another year, and besides, this housefly was every minute decreasing the price he might expect to receive for his beautiful figurine.

"The confectioner came to the window and swatted mightily at the housefly with a rolled-up paper. Although the housefly was not fleet, he atoned for his lack of speed by being ever vigilant. He always looked for an attack from the confectioner, so when the attack came, he was prepared, and flew away before the confectioner could come out from behind his counter.

"This went on for days. It grew late in the year for the housefly to remain, but love for the little figurine sustained him and gave him the strength to go on. They were great friends, and though he wished there could be something more than simple friendship between them, the mere friendship of such a wonderful creature was enough to keep him.

"Meanwhile, the confectioner was worried that the housefly had chased away all interest in his figurine. He was quite reconciled to the idea of selling her now, and had very much convinced himself that this was the only reason he had created her in the first place.

"The confectioner considered how he would raise interest in her once again. Finally, he came to an idea. He spoke his idea tenderly to the little woman in the window. 'How would you like it if I made a husband and children for you?' he asked. 'Wouldn't that be nice? An entire family of sugar. Who could resist? Would you like that, huh?' And he smiled very pleasantly at her, as if he did not have his own reasons for giving her a family.

"The figurine was delighted at the idea of having a husband and children to love. It was the most wonderful thing that could happen, even to a woman made of sugar. She wanted to burst with happiness, but she was only a figure made of sugar, so she said nothing, and only looked back at the confectioner with that same wistful smile she wore since she was first molded.

"Next day, the housefly came back to buzz around and protect her, as was his happy duty. But the housefly was distracted today, for there was something heavy on his mind. At last, he could contain himself no longer. His love spilled out to the figurine. 'Oh, how I love you!' he declared to her. 'If only you would say you love me too, we could be so happy with each other. We could be married, and then we would certainly live happily ever after.' There. He had said it. Now he trembled as he awaited the result of his words.

"The beautiful little figurine cast her eyes away from him. 'Oh housefly,' she said. 'You are my dearest friend in all the world. There is nothing I would trade for your friendship. But we could never be married, for we are of different worlds. A cast of sugar and a housefly are not meant for each other. Indeed, I am to be given a husband and family of sugar, like myself. The confectioner has told me so.' The figurine tried to look sad and happy all at once so the housefly would understand her position.

"The housefly did understand, and somewhere deep within him, he knew she was right. But that did not stop his heart from breaking.

"The figurine felt his pain. 'I'm so sorry to hurt you, my friend. Do you think you could be happy for me?' she asked.

"The housefly perked himself up. 'Yes. Of course I am happy for you. I'm your friend; I'll serve whatever cause brings you happiness,' he told her.

"Soon after, the confectioner kept his promise by bringing to the window figurines of a man and children. He placed them expertly so there could be no doubt of the delicious happiness of the family. The figures gazed lovingly at each other, but it was not just show. They were truly happy together, as only those meant for each other can be.

"The housefly saw this, and it brought him consolation. If the one he loved most were happy, then he would find his contentment in that. He would support her happiness with every means at his disposal. He never spoke of love to her again. Instead he did everything to lead her to believe he was satisfied with only friendship, so she soon forgot all about his foolish profession of love to her.

"Interest in the figurines grew, now that there was a happy family of them. But the interest of likely customers fell again as they saw a

179

late-season housefly buzzing around the group. The confectioner's ire grew taller than ever, but the housefly kept up a constant watch and he always escaped to safety before the confectioner could harm him.

"And so, no one ever bought the beautiful little family of sugar. At length, the confectioner moved them out of the window and stored them someplace where no customers would see them anymore. Now they could live without any fear of being eaten up.

"The housefly was lonely to see them go, but he felt happy that he had helped save them. Now, at last he could rest. The little figurine he loved so well, and those who were foremost to her, were safe. He had done his duty.

"The confectioner never was able to swat the housefly, but the confectioner was not the gravest danger. Winter was near. A housefly may defy the chill of autumn, but he is no match for the cold of winter.

"And so the housefly prepared to say goodbye to the world. He was content with his life. Though he was slow and lived in a world with no one who would see him as a peer, though his existence meant nothing to the whole world, he was content with the course of his life, for he had loved deeply and devoted all of himself to his love.

"The end of his life found him at peace, because of how he had spent it. People thought him little more than a nuisance of a housefly, who did nothing more than turn them away from sweet treats. But he had been a creature with a purpose, and he had served that purpose faithfully. He had spent his life the only way he would have wanted to: in service to the one he loved. And no one ever knew."

Anders gazed up over the children's heads to where the night met the sunset. He stared at the thin line between darkness and light. He whispered toward that place where the earth met sky, "And no one ever knew."

Chapter 40

When the story ended, Anders said goodnight to the children and sent them off to bed. Then he turned to Sister Katrine, who had been as faithful a listener as the children over the years. The nun was still a young woman, though any likeness to childhood had faded. She had taken on a motherly role with the children, just as Anders was like a grandfather to them.

"I wish you would take a message to Sister Clem for me," Anders said.

"Of course," she agreed, "but would you not rather speak to her yourself?"

Anders gave her a wistful smile. "I would like to, but I'm afraid that would be too inconvenient just now."

"Very well. What shall I tell her?"

Anders looked into her eyes. His eyes beamed satisfaction and gratitude. "Just this. Tell her 'Thank you.' Tell her I said 'Thank you for allowing me an hour with the children every day. They have been the most rewarding hours, filled with more love than any man could ask.' That's all."

Sister Katrine nodded.

"And Sister," Anders went on. "I hope you will always continue to be a great friend and guide to these children."

"I will be as much a friend to them as I have the power to be."

Anders nodded with a soft smile. "I'm happy to know they will always have such a kind and generous friend."

"In that, I'll always be second to you," she said.

"There is no rank among those who give all they can. You are a first-rate example of goodness and charity."

"Only because I had a first-rate teacher."

"Indeed. Sister Clem deserves high praise."

"I wasn't speaking of Sister Clem. Well, goodnight, Anders."

"Good night, Sister Katrine," he replied. When she had turned

181

and taken a few steps away, he whispered, "And goodbye."

Retiring to his cottage, Anders locked the door, a thing he rarely did. He wished not to be disturbed, as it was a singular evening.

The light Anders saw under the closed door in his mind did not fade this time as it had always done at the end of one of his stories. This time, the light grew brighter. It reached around the bottom corner of the door and spread up the crack at the side. Soon, it had rounded another corner and spread itself along the top of the door, growing brighter all the while.

Anders took pen and paper and wrote down the story he had just told the children, as he did each night. The words flowed from the pen as if it were a river and the paper were the sea, waiting to collect the stream of waters creation had meant for it. Anders, held rapt by the brilliant light within his mind, hardly thought of the writing at all.

At last, the writing was finished. Though Anders had never done such a thing before, he signed his name to the bottom of the last sheet. Then he added the papers to the stacks of others, filled with the many years' worth of fairy tales he'd told to generations of children. It was a considerable collection. He carefully made the assemblage tidy before putting away his pen and ink.

When this was done, he went to his bedroom and removed from the bottom of his chest a very old suit of clothes. The suit was out of date, but it had been so well cared for that, except for its old-fashioned cut, it might have been stitched together that day. Anders thoroughly brushed down the suit. When he was satisfied, he took off his garden clothes and dressed himself in the suit, making himself as presentable as he could.

When Anders was done dressing, he sat on his bed. That was not enough. He lay down, concentrating all his energy on the light within his mind. He watched. It was brighter than it had ever been before, and closer.

The light at the top and bottom of the door fused with the light at the side so that the corners were no longer discernible. After so many years of being locked and out of reach, the door opened.

Anders went toward the doorway. It did not recede as it always had in the past. It stayed, and the light from beyond drove the shadows from his face for the very first time. In that light he saw everything. Everything he had once known, everything he had ever loved, was in the light. And now, at last, he was in the light too.

The light spread over his entire body. He moved forward. Now he was at the door. He was at the long lost door to everything. He stepped again. Now he was through the doorway. Anders became the light. At last, he was where he belonged. Anders was whole once more.

CHAPTER 41

Next morning, Anders could not be found. The children searched the grounds but he was nowhere. They pounded at his door with their little fists, but there was no answer. The children ran to the nuns for help. The nuns always knew the right thing to do when something was amiss.

The children first came to Sister Clemence. This was fortunate, as Sister Clem was the most resourceful nun. She had helped the children many times before when their troubles had outmatched their abilities. But in this dilemma, even the genius of Sister Clem was tested, for she could accomplish nothing by pounding at Anders's door either.

In her wisdom, she searched for a key, but even this sensible act would not answer. It had been so long since anyone had needed a key to Anders's door that no one knew where one was to be found. Having a key to Anders's door was like keeping extra dirt, in case the children ever ran out of it behind their ears; it was something no one had ever imagined would be necessary. That the door should be locked filled everyone with a sense of foreboding.

At length, Sister Clem found something almost as good as a key. This was Anders's young assistant gardener, who had strong arms and broad shoulders. At Sister Clem's behest, he threw his broad shoulders at Anders's door. The weak bolt was no match for his brawn, and the door gave way.

They rushed into the cottage, but found no trace of Anders in the front rooms. Not until they came to his bedroom did they see him. He lay on his bed, dressed in a decades-old wedding suit. He appeared peacefully asleep. But it was the sleep that only comes at the end of life. The work of Anders Christiansen was done.

There is an old bit of lore about Anders Christiansen that lives to this day. It says that when he was found lying on his bed that morning, there was also found, held over his heart by a lifeless hand, a very old letter. The letter was written in the flowery hand of a young woman. It explained that the reason she could never fall in love with him was due to blemishes in her own character, not his. It was yellow with age, yet very carefully creased and well cared for. After all these years, no one has ever proved the truthfulness of this legend, yet somehow it is not difficult to believe.

Chapter 42

A little chapel was built on the school grounds when the Church first took possession of them. In this chapel the nuns planned a small funeral for Anders. It was to be a humble gardener's funeral—a short, private ceremony that would allow the children of the school to pay their respects but not take too much time away from their studies. The school would say goodbye to the man for an hour or so, then he would be taken to the cemetery and life would continue for the rest. This was what the nuns had envisioned.

As the funeral hour approached, Sister Katrine ran to the school from the chapel. She found Sister Clemence consulting with the priest who came to say the Funeral Mass. "Forgive the interruption, Father," she apologized, attempting to remain respectful though her cheeks were flushed from running and her voice cracked with excitement. "Sister," she gasped, "there is something you may want to see!"

In past times, Sister Clem would have scolded a subordinate for interrupting in such an unruly way. But the years had softened Sister Clem's rigidity, in posture and in personality. "What is it, Sister?" she asked, showing only mild annoyance.

Sister Katrine struggled to articulate her thoughts. "People! Scads of them! Oh, I can't describe it. Please do come see for yourself!"

Shadows of Sister Clem's old impatience showed in her face. She turned toward the priest. "I'm sorry, Father. Will you excuse me for a moment?"

"I'll walk with you, if you don't mind," the priest said.

Sister Katrine led them out of the building. Her excited gait tried to prod them into hurrying, but she could not influence the dignified pace of her superiors. Sister Clem was used to young people becoming excited over things that were of no consequence. It was enough that she would investigate the cause of Sister Katrine's excitement; there was no need to overexert herself.

Besides, they walked through the beautiful gardens Anders had kept for them. Sister Clem was proud of the gardens. She hoped the priest would notice their beauty. Perhaps he would comment about it in his discussions with other officials of the Church.

The way led them to the chapel from the rear. Sister Katrine took them around the side of the building until they could see the path to its front door. As the scene unfolded before them, the mouths of both Sister Clem and the priest fell agape. "What is this?" the priest asked as his eyes followed the scene from left to right.

Sister Clem smiled, but only to herself. What she saw before her would be a great inconvenience to her plans for the funeral. Once, that would have mattered to her. Today, it did not. Today, Sister Clemence experienced another rare moment when she understood she'd made a mistake. Her plans for the funeral had been ill-conceived. As on a former occasion, the ones whom the gardener had touched showed her the error.

"This, Father," she replied, "is what I believe is called a legacy."

From the doorway of the chapel, a line of people wound through the gardens until it was lost behind a distant row of high hedges. There were men and women of all ages, from all walks of life. There were children too. Together, they stood with a somber patience, waiting to pay their respects. They had not come for a gardener's funeral; they had come out of respect for a man who had shone the great light of inspiration upon all of their imaginations at one time or another.

Word of the funeral had gotten out to the town. From there it had spread along the very same binding threads of humanity this man had weaved with his little stories. People all over the country heard the news, and they remembered him. They remembered when they were children and lived in his town. They remembered sitting and listening to him tell his stories. And they remembered the spells those stories had cast over them.

They were spells of hope or courage or confidence, or whatever inspiration children might need to overcome what troubled them. The people remembered the stories and the spells and the inspirations, and above all these things they remembered the great love for all people behind every one of them.

Some were older and some were younger, but they had all been children once. Among them were those who were children still. Some of these had heard stories directly from Anders's mouth. Others had only heard his stories as their parents remembered them, there being in the procession many who repeated Anders's stories to their children in hopes of sharing the delights of their own youth.

Sister Clem had soothed one weeping child after another since the moment Anders was found. Now she noticed the same moist eyes and sniffling nose beside her as Sister Katrine struggled to keep composed. "Did he remind you of your grandfather, too?" Sister Clem asked.

"I never knew a grandfather," Sister Katrine replied as the tears spilled down her cheeks. "Until him."

The people filed through the chapel all day and into the night. To be sure, there were tears shed, and also smiles as they remembered the pleasures of being whisked away into Anders's make-believe worlds. It was the finest remembrance ever paid a simple gardener.

Chapter 43

At last, Anders was taken away to the cemetery for proper burial and the nuns returned to the business of schooling the children. All that remained was to dispose of Anders's few worldly possessions. Ordinarily, this would have been a simple matter of calling in his next of kin to carry away anything of value. Since Anders had no known relatives, this presented a minor dilemma.

Suzette had been traveling abroad at the time of Anders's death, and had missed his funeral. This circumstance caused her great regret, which she attempted to assuage by visiting Anders's gravesite at the earliest opportunity. She stopped to pay her respects to the nuns who had employed Anders for so many years. In doing so, she solved their dilemma of how to dispose of the gardener's effects, readily agreeing to accept them all.

Suzette easily found places about her home for all the small remembrances of her childhood friend. She was unprepared, however, for the wealth of papers filled with fairy tales. She had never dreamt of their existence. She read through all of the handwritten pages, from the story of the sweetest rose, which she remembered so well, through to the latest stories, where the ink seemed still fresh.

Memories of childhood with Anders and Elsa flooded over her. She remembered listening to Anders's little stories, and how they always helped her to look at the world in different ways. Whether they were happy tales or ones that were a little bit sad, those stories always made her feel better about her troubles. Anders had a gift for making everyone feel better.

When Suzette reached the last story, the tale about the housefly in autumn, she was torn between a smile and a tear. In this story, she saw the truth. There was a truth in all of Anders's stories, but this truth touched her more closely. Only she could know the depth of this truth.

Suzette had grandchildren now, and when she finished crying, she read Anders's stories to them. They took great delight in the tales.

189

After each one, they clamored for another. Then, after all the stories had been read, they begged to hear their favorites again and again.

Her grandchildren's response to Anders's stories brought a notion to her mind. She was determined not to let these stories lie where future generations would not benefit from a simple, truthful mind and an always-giving heart. At once she began a quest to find a publisher.

She went from one to the next until she found one willing to try the stories on his own children. It did not take long for him to see how his own children fell in love with the words of Anders Christiansen. In short order, a bargain was struck. The first bound book of Anders's stories was printed and made available to the public. The fairy tales of Anders Christiansen were in print, where they have been ever since.

Today a statue of Anders Christiansen rises up from the fountain in the square of the town where he lived. The people of that place look up at the statue with pride, eager to claim Anders Christiansen as their greatest treasure. No one talks about the slowness of his speech. They only say that he was the greatest writer of children's stories who ever lived, and that he was one of their own. He was one of their own, but now he belongs to children everywhere.

There are few, in all of the world, who do not know at least some of the tales of Anders Christiansen. His stories shape the lessons of childhood. As grown-ups, we understand how much they are fantasy. Those who retain some youthful imagination may return to them once in a while as a refuge from the complexities of the world.

Some are flights of fancy we only wish could be real. Others are unreached glories that withered on the vine and tripped us, bringing us crashing to earth. They are wishes upon stars that fell a thousand years ago. Yet, they make us keep just one more wish to place upon a likely star. That is their greatest value to us.

But they are nothing more than dreams.

Some dreams present themselves as lofty expectations, pursued in hopes of becoming what we think we are meant to be. Other dreams are a mired existences, from which we only wish to awaken and be set free to redeem our expectations. When life is disrupted by this kind of dream, the decision must be made whether to live in loathing of the dream or to set to work building new dreams, no matter how humble. This is the challenge and the choice with dreams.

Anders Christiansen made his choice, though he could not have known its legacy. Had he surrendered to anger over the loss of his grandest expectations, his name would be erased from history. Instead, he set to work building new dreams. They were small dreams, but the generosity with which he shared them allowed them to grow with time. This is what can be done with small dreams.

Anders Christiansen's tales are great escapes that began as small dreams. As he predicted to his professors one rainy afternoon, they are "Only just dreams."

THE END

AUTHOR'S POSTSCRIPT:

Is this story actually about Hans Christian Andersen? The answer to that question is mostly no. All characters and events of this novel are purely fictional. This story is not about Hans Christian Andersen, but it was inspired in part by his fairy tales. Although it is not a biography of that great storyteller, it is my hope that this story captures, however imperfectly, the spirit of Hans Christian Andersen's gifts to the collective imagination of humanity.

Made in the USA
San Bernardino, CA
11 June 2015